GW00455482

UNLAWFUL

YOUNG OUTLAWS MC BOOK 1

TL WAINWRIGHT

YOUNG OUTLAWS MC
UNLAWFUL
Book one

First edition. March 2020
© 2020 T.L Wainwright

This is a work of fiction. The names, characters, places, and incidents are products of the writer's imagination or have been used fictitiously and are not to be construed as real. Any resemblance to persons, living or dead, actual events, locales or organisations is entirely coincidental. All rights reserved.

No part of this publication may be reproduced, distributed, or transmitted in any form or by any means, including photocopying, recording, or other electronic or mechanical methods without the prior written permission of the publisher except for brief quotations embodied in critical reviews
Thank you.

Story Editor:
Jackie McLeish
Nikki Young

edited by:
Eleanor Lloyd-Jones

Cover:
Francessca's PR & Designs

Formatting by:
Graphic Shed

✿ Created with Vellum

PROLOGUE

"Please, Remy, they're too young. They shouldn't live here—be around all this violence. If we bought the house, then..."

"Shut the fuck up, woman," he growls back. "Is that what you want: have them living in a little house with a picket fence, reading and playing with a fucking train set?"

"They need their childhood, not all this..." Ma waves her hand around the bar at the guys with women dressed in tiny skirts and bras that hardly cover their bodies draped around them, the aroma of stale beer and sex lingering in the air.

My father jumps up from the wing-backed chair that everyone treats like it's his throne and grabs my mother by the throat. He pulls her close to him, their faces nearly touching. He's not a tall man by any means, but he makes up for it with girth. My ma, who is no more than five feet tall, is left with her feet barely touching the floor as he hisses into her face.

"What are you trying to say, woman?" Spit sprays from his snarling mouth. "This is where I was brought up as a child. In this very room. Are you disrespecting my parents?"

"No, Remy, I didn't mean that. I just..."

"Let me make this clear, bitch. I intend to bring up my boys the way I was. They will live in this club house, be a part of the MC, until I feel that they are ready to officially become one of the Young Outlaws. You get me?"

"Yes," my mother whispers.

"I can't hear you," he snarls with his free hand cupping the shell of his ear. It's loud enough for all the guys to hear him and is met with a shower of laughter.

"Yes, Remy," she repeats, this time louder. When he pushes her away, her arms flay at her side as she endeavors to regain her balance. When she does, she stands firm with an air of stubbornness, her head held high and a look of determination on her face, not wanting to show any sign of weakness. The single tear that I see track down her cheek before she quickly turns and walks away betrays her true feelings.

"My boys will not grow up to be pussies," he shouts after her before turning his attentions back to *the club members and laughs. "The only pussy they will be interested in is the kind they'll find between some club whore's thighs."*

His boys!

What a fucking joke.

CHAPTER ONE

I'm Cannon. Well, that's my club name and what most people know me by, but my real name is Colt. I'm the youngest of three all-male siblings. My two older brothers are twins: Smith and Wesson, Wes for short. Yes, my pa is a fucking gun nut as was his father before him—not that I ever knew my grandfather: he had been shot in the head by a disgruntled, bent cop who was none too happy about being taken off the MC's payroll.

Smith had been the first of my father's heirs to be born into the MC way of life and, according to Ma, had been in one hell of a rush to make an appearance, sliding out like he was coated in butter. Wesson not so much. Having a home birth in the Young Outlaws MC club house was never a good idea but was one that my father was insistent on and, as always, his orders were abided by.

Wes was big—so big that Ma had struggled to birth him, and when he'd eventually arrived, he was blue. Story has it that amongst the gut-wrenching cries of my mother, Ratchet—one of the club whores —performed in a way that nobody knew was possible at such a young age. Blowies yes, CPR not so much, but she worked on Wes and astounded everyone when she brought the life back into him. Turned out that nineteen-year-old Lisa—re-named by the guys due to the fact that she was as sexy as sin and could tighten anyone's nuts—had been training to be a nurse before she got caught up with the club. Her fledgling career had taken a nosedive when she got kicked out for screwing one of the married docs. Their loss was our gain.

After that, Lisa gained a lot of respect both from the club members and my Ma. If someone got hurt or sick, nurse Ratchet had been called in. She'd even become a dab hand with a needle and thread, but that's another story.

At the side of his twin, Smith, it had become clear that Wes's development was much slower, which had concerned Ma but hadn't stop her loving him any less.

While Smith had been running around hyper at

eighteen months, Wes had still been shuffling around on his ass. Talking hadn't come easy for him either. Even to this day, his speech is a little slow, which gives people the impression that he's just some thick retard. Oh, how fucking wrong are they. Wes is so fucking bright, and his artwork astounds me, yet people don't see past the big monster of a man, or the way he speaks: slow, clear and precise. He's hard as nails, but only the ones close to him know that hiding within him is a heart of pure gold.

So as not to confuse the shit out of you, let me explain the club members, our biker names and the screwed-up reasoning behind them.

Bullet – President

Of course, this is my pops, the President of the Young Outlaws, whose actual biker name is Bullet, an obvious choice with his official name being Remington Gunner. Everyone just calls him Pres, or Boss and sometimes asshole... but only behind his back.

Gearhead – Sgt at Arms – newly appointed.

An ex-marine with a knowledge of mechanics that would put Nikola Tesla to shame. Bikes, motor vehicles... damn, he could even re-build a semi if we needed him to.

· · ·

Conda – Secretary and Treasurer because members are limited.

Don't get giddy girls: his name has nothing to do with the size of his trouser snake. In fact, we don't know much about Conda's history other than he was apparently the unexpected result of a split condom. His underaged mother had given him up, and with no family willing to take him, he'd ended up a son of the state and ping-ponged around various undesirable foster homes. At least when he became an adult, he found a permanent family: The Young Outlaws Motorcycle Club.

Masher – Enforcer

Big fucker built like a tank and with a punch that's equivalent to being hit by a freight train. Enough said.

Buzz – Member

This guy might have a hand missing, but he's as dexterous as any other man and has a determination beyond any other. His loss of limb was not from combat but from a freak accident with a chainsaw. Less questions asked the better.

· · ·

Mac – Member

After leaving the military, the only work he'd been able to get was working at a McDonalds drive thru. One day, he'd just happened to get talking with Gearhead, swapping combat stories, and they'd clicked. Decision made. The club had better job prospects.

JB or Johny Bravo – Member

Named after the cartoon character because he's a pretty boy who wants nothing more than to impress the girls. But 'Whoa, Mama!' you'd be more than happy to have him watching your back as long as there're no ladies in the vicinity.

Creeper - Member

Now this guy is a creepy fucker. It's not just the fact that he watches every move like he's an FBI agent, but he appears out of nowhere when you least expect it. He even scares the shit out of me.

Tag-it – Member

Loves to fuck ladies tag team style with Creeper.

· · ·

Toothpick – Prospector

Tall, skinny guy that has only just patched in from another charter of the YOMC. It was them who gave him his name, so don't blame me. I'm not the type to give someone grief about their stature.

We have a couple more Prospectors, but as yet they're still pretty insignificant until they've proven themselves.

Then we have the club whores. There're quite a few that come and go, but the three main club ladies are...

Nails – JoJo.

Fingernails always painted the bloodiest red, always long and pointed, and if you ask her nicely, she'll tear the hell out of your back while you shoot your load into her pussy or between her talented lips.

Ratchet – Lisa

Well, you already know how she got her name.

.   .   .

Poison - Veronica

This bitch should have a neon sign permanently suspended right above her head. 'Don't trust this woman' because everything she touches goes to shit, and unfortunately, she has her sights on me. Bitch with a capital B.

When it came to the President's sons, a club name had been bestowed upon each of us even before we'd been able to ride a bike. I've never been one-hundred percent sure if it was actual club etiquette, but as we were the Presidents kids, who was going to argue? If it hadn't been for Smith's mischievousness, then it might not have come about until we were much older, but when it had gone to church and put to the vote, each of our names had been decided with the crash of the gavel.

Smith had been the first to be given his official club name at the tender age of nine. After being dared by both Wes and me, he'd jumped on one of the prospector's rides, only to lose control of the heavy, powerful Harley and crash it into the wall of the outbuilding. Pops had thought it was hilarious, the Prospector not so much as his ride had been a fucking mess. Smith had just spat the brick dust from his mouth and brushed the rubble from his clothes and hair. As it turned out, the building had ended up needing some repair work too.

"That's my fucking son!" Pops hollers, a rare shimmer of pride in his voice. "Tougher than a mother-fucking brick wall."

Brick had been given a prospector cut the very next day, although he wasn't put through the usual hazing shit that the rest of the prospectors had to go through. That didn't come until a good few years later.

If Smith had his MC tag, then being his twin, it had only been right that Wes should get his, too.

Mammoth—it had to be. Even at such a young age, he'd been built like a huge fucking mammal, and he'd had such thick, dark hair. Even his face had fuzz. It had been clear even then he was going to be a hairy motherfucker.

After I'd griped and moaned like a chicken shit kid—well, I was only eight—I got my own name, too.

At my birth, my pops had glanced at me lying on a towel as Ratchet sponged me down to remove all the blood and crap off me. He had shouted at the top of his voice, "Well the little bastard has nuts as big as cannon balls, but his dick, it's just a teenie, weenie peenie. He's gonna be fucked if it doesn't grow along with him." Let's just say that when it had come to picking my MC name, it was that particular comment all those years before that had got me the tag of Cannon Balls, which over time has been cut to just Cannon. Although, I'm pleased to say that my balls are still big, and my cock has grown into one huge fucking weapon.

I'd come along eleven months after Smith and Wesson, which meant my pops hadn't even let my ma get her breath back before he'd been rutting into her again. Dirty bastard.

Although there's very little age difference between us, Smith has taken the role of big brother very seriously over the years, protecting Wes and me equally with a ferocity that is unyielding. When we were younger, he would constantly try and put himself between us and Pops, but not one of us would back away. It hadn't mattered whichever one of us three brothers it was that was in the firing line for pissing the old man off: we would stand together, take on and share the burden of his wrath.

Some of the club members had thought that my Pops' level of discipline was acceptable. Hell, it's probably because they were brought up the same way. Others, well, they'd turned and walked away, knowing that if they interjected then they would then have become the victim. The punishment of going against the Pres had ranged between a bout in the makeshift boxing ring with Masher—believe me, you don't want that: he is a fucking six-foot-five animal with a chest span the size of a semi-truck who leaves everyone he fights in a shit heap of a mess, or a hair's breadth from death once he's played with them for thirty minutes or so—and (if he was really pissed and that way out) looking down the barrel of The Pres's own favorite 38-caliber Colt Cobra special... the same gun that was used to shoot Lee Harvey Oswald back in 1963; the gun that shot the man, who shot the president of the United States of America. Personally, I have always thought there was more to that story, but Pops has always been insistent that Jack Ruby was a modern-day vigilante of that time.

That just about sums up my childhood. My mother had spent her time trying to shield us from MC life, continuously trying to convince my father to purchase a house where we could live away from debauchery, violence and an illegal lifestyle. However, all she'd got for her incessant nagging was a beating. She'd still always come back for more, though; she'd never given up the fight for her kids.

When I was around thirteen, my mother had started to spend less and less time in the house during the day, despite always being there to get us up in the morning. Breakfast time had always been just the four of us: Ma, Smith, Wesson and me, Colt.

Pops had never been there and neither had any

of the club members. It hadn't been until I was older that I realise that it was because they'd been either unconscious somewhere, sleeping off the previous night's alcohol intake, or still hauled up with one of the club whores getting their dicks wet. Mouth, pussy, ass... whatever.

We would sit around the large table, feasting on a mountain of home cooked food—Ma's pancakes are the best, always piping hot and smothered in the sweetest syrup: Heaven on a plate—and as soon as the plates had been cleared and the kitchen spotless, Ma would leave, but she was always back in the late afternoon when she would cook enough food for the whole club.

Once dinner was done, she would try usher us off to our rooms, only to be overruled by my father. She'd have a different excuse every night as to why we needed to go upstairs, but it had always been a waste of time: what the club Pres says, goes.

Defeated, she would go to their marital bedroom to wait for him—although the chances of my father meeting her in there had been slim. I'd been young but not stupid. It had been clear to me from an early age that my father spent most of his time with his dick in someone else rather than my mother. On the occasion he had stumbled back to their room, the sounds that came from it had had me covering my ears against my mother's cries and pleas to be left alone.

Two days before my fourteenth birthday, my ma hadn't returned in time for dinner. She wasn't there at breakfast either. When Smith had asked Chubs— one of the older members and the only one who seemed to show any concern when it came to Ma—if he'd seen her, he had just shaken his head. Deep sorrow had masked his face when he turned and walked away.

It had been enough to incite Smith to go and face The President himself, our father. Both Wes and I had followed, each of us standing firmly by his side.

Smith and Wes may have been twins, and I guess they've always had a connection that only twins do, but we'd all been close, which was only expected as most of the time, we'd been left to our own devices. If one of us had been in trouble, we'd all been in trouble. We'd covered and stuck up for each other, taking the discipline together.

So, I guess it had been only fitting that when my father had announced with very little emotion that our mother was dead, it had been when we were together, standing in front of the man who suddenly had free rein on our future. How fucking thrilling that was. I can still remember how ridiculous we'd looked: three teenaged boys standing in a row, dressed in jeans and plain black, leather cuts, still, stunned and scared to show any emotion.

We'd got no explanation—no sympathy or signs of sorrow from him. We'd got nothing.

Smith had turned and walked out of the room. We'd followed him across the compound at the back, through the knee-high grass and towards the edge of the swamp.

I'd stood back for a second and watched as Wes walked towards him. As Wes laid a hand on his shoulder, Smith's legs gave way, his knees hitting the ground hard, and the sound of his heart splintering had spilled from his mouth. Just a breath and I'd been by his side, on my knees. Wes, too. We'd fallen into each other, our grief merging into one mountain of pain.

CHAPTER TWO

A war had broken out between Smith and our father. It had been like he was on a suicide mission. If our father had said black, Smith would say white. He'd refused to show him any respect, irrespective of whether it was as his father or the club president. Even if he'd got a beating—at which point, both Wes and me would stand forward in an attempt to take some of his anger—Smith wouldn't show any signs of the pain he undoubtably had been in. He'd been fearless, fierce and unwilling to feed my father's ego, which had only fueled his hatred towards his son. Because that's what it became, mutual hate for each other.

When I hit sixteen, Smith had announced to both me and Wes that he was leaving after a major bust up with Pops. Their relationship had always been bad—as it was with all of us three lads—but with Smith it had been off the chart explosive. On this particular occasion, the punches had come fast and furious, most of them from Smith. He'd totally lost his shit. Each strike with his clenched fist had hit Pop's face and gut hard, fueled by the pent-up pain that had been festering in his head and heart for so long. As much as both Wes and I had pleaded with him to stay, he'd said he couldn't stand to live under the same roof as Pops for much longer.

I can remember like it was yesterday. Not caring that I looked like a pussy, far removed from how the son of a MC President should portray himself, I had been on my knees, begging Smith not to go. No amount of words had been enough to get him to change his mind. In fact, he'd barely been able to look me in the eye as he rebuked my pleas. It had always been on the cards that when the time came, my pops would hand the gavel over to his eldest son, but instead—and to my father's utter disgust—Smith had had other ideas: he joined the marines.

Through all the years, we had stuck together, watched out for each other, but he had turned his back and left us—even his fucking twin, whose bond with him was unearthly. They'd thought the same, felt the same, had had a shit freaky psychic connection that only twins seem to have. Even that hadn't stopped him from abandoning us.

And that is what it had felt like: abandonment.

First, we'd lost Mom—who was our heart, our protector, the light amongst the dark—and as brothers we had become a tight knit unit, closer than ever.

But then, he had been going, too.

My last word to him before he'd mounted his bike had been spat in his face.

'Traitor'.

We'd seen very little of Smith from then on. On the occasion he had ventured home when on leave, he'd opted to stay in a nearby motel, refusing to stay under the same roof as Pops. Our relationship as brothers had been strained, the closeness of our younger years lost. More often than not, he'd make up excuses as to why he couldn't make it back, until eventually, he'd stopped returning home at all.

The club house where we live is well out of town, down a dirt road that is scarcely visible from the main road. Unless you know it is there, you'd have no chance of finding it. Even access from the back is difficult. No one in their right mind would come up through the swamp unless they know the area well, partly due to the fact that it is riddled with gators. Even when the water is high, there is so much shit under there, even the smallest of boats usually ends up getting damaged or grounded. You'd be gator snack in no time. That or simply that you'd be trespassing on Young Outlaws' land. Not a good idea.

It's an old, large, two-story building with a wraparound porch that at one time would have been a beautiful family house. Now, the grey coloured shutters at the windows are aged, the paint cracked and peeling. Most of the woodwork is in desperate need of a lick of fresh paint. The porch that had originally been stained with a dark varnish, is now patchy and worn. Areas are uneven where the planks have broken and been quickly repaired haphazardly with hammer and nail. All in all, the whole place is in desperate need of renovation, but Pops has refused to spend a cent on it. In his eyes, the money that is made from the business, which is mainly from running guns and drugs, needs to be plowed back into the business. Any that is left is spent on liquor, bikes and pussy.

It was back in the 1950's that John James Young, an ex-marine, decided to set up a club. Himself and a handful of his Harley-riding ex-army buddies, one of them being my grandfather, had been at a loose end.

Jobs had been limited and along with that had come depression and a lack of self-worth. Morale amongst them had been at an all-time low. Desperate to put a stop to the rot that was setting in and after hearing about other clubs that had sprung up over the USA, he'd decided to set up the club here in Florida.

At first, they'd picked up jobs for the local haulage firm, fixing vehicles and doing the odd run when they'd been down on drivers. Once they'd had the new premises and land, it had grown from there. When it came apparent that they'd been handling stolen goods anyway, they'd decided they could make more money if they did the dealing themselves. Illegal liquor had come first, which quickly moved on to drugs and then guns. With the acquisition of two storage warehouses, it had grown faster than they'd ever imagined.

At first, they'd been hanging out at one of the local bars, but when John had landed the property after playing a life-changing game of poker, they'd had the perfect place.

The Club House had originally belonged to a local congress man, who had a severe gambling habit and absolutely no self-control. Story has it that John James Young, the founder of the Young Outlaws Motorcycle club, had won it in a very dubious game of poker that has always been shrouded with rumors and myths. I think it had been more a matter of right place, right time and an enormous amount of luck.

Most of the guys had been either single or their marriages were on the rocks. Victims of the pressures and character changes that had been all too familiar from the effects of war. John himself had found that his marriage was nothing but a sham and was the first to move into the club house and take up permanent residence. Soon after, all but two of the ten bedrooms in the house had been taken. The club had expanded fast, the two remaining rooms used on a regular basis for hook-ups. Once the club whores started hanging around, and the heavy drinking had begun, it had only been a matter of time before a fight would break out as to who would get the use of the spare rooms. It hadn't been long before the shenanigans had been spilling out into the living area of the house and nobody seemed to give a damn.

An outbuilding had been erected next to house. That and the two tractor units are still the only visible evidence of what might seem to be a legitimate business. Tools and the equipment required for any repairs are there for all to see, but the pit to get under the vehicles is a different matter. The door inside the pit leads to an underground storage facility. It is undetectable, unless you get down there with a flashlight and have a fucking sixth sense...

The local law had gotten into the club's pocket early on, and with the dollars that the local sheriff has been picking up on a regular basis, the only time they have ever turned up is either at our invitation or after we've been given a tip-off first.

CHAPTER THREE

Business had been good back then. Nowadays, not so much. But Pops is always trying to find a new way of making some extra bucks some of which, I am not okay with.

When the subject of trafficking came up, I'd lost my shit. If Mammoth hadn't have pulled me away from Pops and out of the room, despite the fact that I was brought up to respect the club President, I would have beaten the crap out of him. It's modern-day slavery for fuck's sake, and I hadn't wanted myself or our club dragged into that shit.

I'd known then that I needed to do something to increase the money coming in to ensure that this new, depraved line of business was never taken to church and put to the vote.

Most of the guns we'd been getting were coming from Russia. For some reason, they'd seemed to have a mountain of the fuckers. But getting them in had become increasingly more of a nightmare, which affected our distribution and therefore our cash flow.

The government had stepped up the control at the ports and flying the goods in was too rich and risky for us. So, when Mammoth had Nolan—a high school junky jock—by the throat because he hadn't been able to pay for his five grand coke bill, Jock boy had squealed like a pig. We'd ended up at a condo in Magnolia Pines and coming face to face with an eighteen-year-old kid named Jordan Sparks who had ended up being the answer to all our problems. Nolan had already told us how this Jordan kid was a computer whiz and had managed to make a few of his parking tickets disappear, getting him out of shit city with his father.

If you can hide one thing, then why not something a little bigger? Well, a lot bigger: like a sea container holding a fuckton of guns and ammunition.

With a little heavy persuasion, Jordan had agreed to come on board. I hadn't thought for one minute it had been the money that tempted him into helping us with our problem. It had clearly been the threat of me paying his cute little sister, Leah, a visit sometime to show her a few things was the real reason why he'd agreed to work for us. Not that I would have ever gone through with it. Don't get me wrong, she sure is pretty enough, showing all the signs of being a stunner back then, but she'd been fourteen for fuck's sake. I'd been talking shit to get the result I'd needed. I'm no fucking pedophile.

So, for the past few months, with the help of Jordan's hacking skills, business has been good again. The containers are coming in fast and undetected, which means that our buyers—who are mainly the Irish and Chinese—are happy, too. Neither of them are the easiest to deal with, but personally, it's the Chinese that I fear the most. Maybe I've watched too many martial arts movies, but the last thing I want is to piss of the Triads. They are mean, evil fuckers and there is nothing they won't do to get what they want. And if you disrespect them, well you might as well slit your own throat because what they'll do to you would be without mercy.

So, for the last four of five months, the club has been raking in the money, and with Jordan taking care of the laundering too, the Young Outlaws are fucking reaping the rewards. Thank fuck. The only time the subject of moving bodies comes up now, is when someone has fucked us over and is now sitting in an unmarked grave or has become alligator snacks.

"I've adjusted the chain, but it's still fucking shit

on gear change," Mammoth growls. He's standing looking down at his bike, spinning the key chain around his fat index finger.

"Have you checked the clutch cable?" I ask, bending down and slipping my fingers between the front of the frame to find the inline adjuster. I'm just about to slide off the rubber boot when my phone vibrates in my pocket. When I slip it out of my pocket, the name that's lit up on the screen has me rolling my eyes and cursing under my breath. "Just get Gearhead to take a look at it," I say, dismissing my brother before accepting the call and putting the phone to my ear.

"What can I do for you Officer?"

"Look, the kid, Jordan, he's about to be arrested for computer fraud," the hushed voice speaks quickly.

"When?" I growl down the phone.

"Like now." His voice is barely a whisper.

"Fuck! Why didn't you tell us earlier? At least give us enough time to get him moved."

"Don't you think I would have done if I could? I've only just come on shift and this came out of the blue without any warning." The line goes quiet for a moment other than a faint background noise of voices and people moving about. "Look, he'll be

UNLAWFUL

taken to the station over on Bay Street, but they'll
likely move him to Orlando. That's all I got. I'm
sorry, but I gotta go." The line goes dead.

"Fuck, fuck, fuck," I hiss out between clenched
teeth. Jordan knows too much about the club and
could quite easily feed us to the wolves. The club is
under threat.

I bring up my contact list and stab at the screen
until the phone starts to ring. It gets picked up almost
immediately.

"Luca, Jordan Sparks is just about to be taken in."

"What's the charge?"

"Who gives a fuck? If he starts talking, the club is
dust. You have his details, yeah?"

"I'm pulling them up now. Do you know where
they're taking him?"

"Yeah, Davenport but they'll possibly move him."

"Not till I've seen him they won't," Luca sniggers
down the phone. "I'll make a couple of calls. In the
meantime, you need to come up with a deal that's
going to stop him talking. You're gonna have to think
of something that will guarantee he'll take the fall
and keep the Young Outlaws name out of it."

"Motherfucker!" I grunt, knowing that there's
only one thing that we can possibly use that will
convince Sparks to be the fall guy. A wave of guilt

washes over me, but I know that I need to protect the club.

"Jordan only has one weak spot," I inform Luca. "His sister." As soon as the words leave my mouth, the burner phone I have as a direct line to Jordan pings.

Cops

Holding it in one hand, I punch out my response with my thumb, while still holding the other phone to my ear.

Aware. Don't say a word until your lawyer arrives.

"He's reached out," I tell Luca. "I told him to keep his mouth shut until you get there."

Lawyer?

I reply quickly while listening to Luca.

Courtesy of the Young Outlaws. Destroy the burner now!

"Let's just hope he does because it will make all our lives easier."

Suddenly the background noise becomes louder and it doesn't take a genius to know that Luca is just about to board a chopper. That's another few thousand dollars to the bill.

"I'll send you over a couple of suggestions on how we can play this once I get full information on the arrest so you can run it past Pres, and we'll talk later.

Luca Rossi, attorney at law, well-dressed gentleman and as bent as shit. Tall, dark with an air of dominance about him. His Italian ancestry screams from every pore of his skin. Whether he was linked to the Mafia or not, I've no idea, but it wouldn't be a surprise if I found out he was.

I still don't know to this day how or why he became involved with the club, but he did. Whenever I'd brought up the subject with Pops, he'd quickly shoot it down, a face on him like a slapped ass for days after. It had got to the point where I just stopped asking.

Clenching my fist, I smash it into the screen of the burner phone before launching it into the concrete ground. I drop my head back and scream at the sky. "Motherfucker!"

"Is it really that bad?" Mammoth questions at my outburst. I give him the rundown of my conversations with both the cop and Luca.

"Why is it when everything seems to be running along so fucking smoothly, it all turns to shit? How the fuck are we going to get the containers in now? Pops is going to lose his shit."

"We'll just have to find a way to make money elsewhere."

My brother—ever the optimist. But the 'else-where' that the Pres will be wanting to branch out to, is sick as fuck: a road I don't want the club to go down. We flaunt ourselves in front of the law far too much as it is.

Once we call Church, it isn't long before we have a unanimous vote on the offer that we were going to put forward to Jordan Sparks. As usual, Pops loses it, blaming me for getting involved with Jordan in the first place. Funny how he hasn't been complaining about the fuckton of cash that has been coming in over the past months, though.

It's around thirty minutes after Rossi arrived at the precinct that we hear back from him.

"You were right about his weak spot. I didn't mention her, but he came back with a condition, and for him, it's a deal breaker: he wants his sister protected, and he means protected. So, you'd better make sure that whoever it is you have watching her, even the prospectors, don't put their grubby hands on her either. She's off limits to everyone, even your fucking father. You understand me?"

"Sure." I laugh at Jordan's ridiculous demands.

"I'm fucking damn serious, Cannon," Luca growls down the phone. "He's passionate about this. No shitting you, I could see it in the fucker's eyes. Leah is all he has left, and if you let anything happen to her, and I mean anything, he'll be at the nearest precinct singing like Celine Dion at Caesar's Palace, meaning you and the rest of the YOMC will be the ones doing time."

That's all I fucking need: to be babysitting a hormonal teenager. "Okay, okay. I got yah."

"And one other thing," he adds.

"And what's that?"

"When he gets out, he's no longer in debt to the MC."

"You've got to be fucking kidding me. How the hell do we know he's not going to just fuck us over when he gets out?"

"Don't worry. I've got plans for Jordan Sparks. He won't be a problem."

"How can you be so sure?"

"Have I ever let you down?" he adds. "Trust me."

"I'm not sure who's got who by the balls here." I growl out.

"It's not about who has the upper hand here: it's about protecting the club."

"I need to take this to vote."

"You don't have fucking time. You need to make the decision, Cannon. Let's be honest, your father might be the Pres, but it's you that the runs this shit show."

I hear the sound of a zipper going down and then running water.

"Are you taking a piss?"

"Might be. Anyway, don't change the subject. Do I go back and tell him he's got a deal?"

"Yeah, he's got a deal."

CHAPTER FOUR

One Year later

It's already been a year of this babysitting shit, and although most of the time I put one of the prospectors onto it, occasionally, like today, I do a shift or two. Why? Because I have this indescribable sense of being indebted to Sparks. Also, I want to make sure there're no fuckups with the updates we send monthly via Rossi. Sparks needs to be sure that we're sticking to our side of the deal.

It pisses me off that some computer-hacking geek of a fucker has this hold over the club. Even though business had been good for a while, it'd been a mistake bringing in that clever little asshole. While ever Jordan is still inside, there's that risk he could squeal, so the sooner he's released, the better. His sister will then become his responsibility, too, and no longer mine. Halle-fucking-lujah.

Leaning against my ride, I light up another smoke while watching the entrance door of the Walgreens store situated at the other side of the road. I'd watched her go in there nearly an hour ago, her high, blonde ponytail swishing side to side with her confident swagger. Just how fucking long does it take a chick to pick up a few groceries? I flick some of the ash from my smoke into the palm of my hand and run it over my newly attached V. President badge to dirty up the white stitching. Pops had made me up following my predecessor checking out after getting caught up in the crossfire between the YOMC and a rival club over turf ground.

I mumble a 'halle-fucking-lujah' under my breath when I see the door swing open, and she steps out onto the pavement. Daylight is fading fast, but I can tell it's her from the bright yellow of her fitted tank top and black yoga pants that show that, even at only sixteen, her body is tight and has curves in the right places. I continue to watch her as she starts to make her way down the sidewalk in the direction of where she lives. Home for her is with Sheila Fenwick.

After the loss of their parents, Sparks had been granted guardianship of his sister, and even a hard bastard like me finds it difficult not to feel for the fucker. That shit must have been hard: eighteen, no parents and having to look after a fourteen-year-old hormonal teenager. When Sparks had been taken into custody, Old Lady Fenwick, a co-worker and good friend of their parents, had taken Leah in and had been there ever since, after more tragedy hit the family. The only remaining family member, their English grandmother had passed away on the very day Sparks received his sentence. Unlucky as fuck.

I flick my cigarette to the curb and get on my bike because it's only a matter of time before I'll lose sight of her when she turns the corner at the end of the street. I'm just about to kick the standoff when she stops dead in her tracks where there is a gap between the buildings. I can almost hear her thoughts as she looks down the alleyway then up the main street, debating whether to take the short cut or the safer, longer option to get home.

"Don't do it," I mumble to myself. "Be a good girl and stay on the main street."

She takes a couple of steps forward and I think she's made the right decision, but then she spins on her heels and walks into the alleyway, disappearing out of sight.

"Aww fuck this shit!"

I kick back the stand, start up my ride and pull back on the throttle. I need to move fast so I can get to the other side before she does. I just hope that she doesn't run it, or worse still, take another detour on route, because if she does, I'll lose her.

Thankfully I don't hit any red lights or traffic, and I get to where I need to be in record time. I pull the bike up just right of the opening and wait. In my head, I try and judge the time it will have taken for her to walk through, and by my reckoning, she should be coming out any second.

I wait and wait, but there's still no sign of her. Maybe she ran. But even if she did, I would have caught sight of her further down the sidewalk before she slipped into her house.

My back stiffens and my gut becomes tight. Something doesn't feel right.

Dismounting my bike, I secure it and slip off my helmet, leaving it hooked over one of the handlebars before making my way into the alley. I don't get far before I hear a noise that sounds like scuffling feet a little further up. A deep hiss of a voice telling someone to 'shut the fuck up' can be heard from the other side of a dumpster. Immediately, I'm on high alert. I hear a muffled whimper, and I know instinctively who it is. Rage builds within me at an alarming speed, and I move quickly but stealth-like until I'm right up behind him with my arm around his neck and my knife already piercing the fabric of his hoody.

"Let her go," I growl into his ear, "or I'll cut you so deep your guts will be painting the sidewalk red and the rest of your sorry ass will be in the dumpster." I put a little more pressure on the blade so he doesn't misunderstand my threat. He releases his hold on her and she falls to the floor. Spinning him around, I push his back against the wall, my hand tight around his throat. Glancing down, I find his pants are open, and his semi-hard cock is hanging out. I take a step back, so his dick doesn't make contact with me but don't release my hold on him. In fact, on realizing his intent—what he was about to do to her—I tighten my grip until he's red in the face and choking for breath.

"You dirty fucking cunt," I spit at him. My fist makes contact with his face with such force that the back of his head hits hard against the brick wall. It's enough to render him unconscious, and I launch him to the ground. Standing over him, I'm ready to continue with my beating until desperate cries from Leah grab my attention and have me snapping out of my rage.

Hunched on the floor, she clutches desperately to the torn neckline of her tank, her hands pulling at her yoga pants as she tries to get them back up, but with her legs tucked under her, its difficult for her to cover herself. A scrap of black lace fabric is on the floor beside her, her panties ripped from her young, innocent body.

I've done some sick and twisted stuff in my life, but she's a kid for fuck's sake. The urge to cut the motherfucker that did this starts to rise again, but instead I put my hand out to her. As soon as it comes to rest on her shoulder, she screams, and backs up further against the wall.

"Hey, it's okay," I say, pulling my hand back and holding it up, palm to her, as a sign that I mean her no harm. "I'm not going to hurt you."

She looks at me wide-eyed, a gentle crease appearing on her forehead as she tries to work out if she can trust me or not. When she starts to pull at her pants again, this time with both hands, the fabric of her vest falls forward, leaving her pert breast exposed. She whimpers out in frustration as she tries desperately to regain some dignity.

"Wait a minute." I go to put my hands on hers to still them but think better of it. Instead I stand up, slip off my cut and tuck it between my knees while I pull my T-shirt over my head. "Here, put this on." I hand her my black, classic Harley shirt, and when she looks me in the eye, I see pain, humiliation and gratitude.

"Take it."

When she still doesn't move, I crouch down in front of her.

"Can I help you put it on?"

When she gives me a gentle nod, I hunch up the shirt and slide it over her head. I watch the emotions transpire on her face as she fights to hold back tears. I gently pull the fabric down until it covers her enough that she can slip one of her arms in. With a quick twist to her side, she leans her upper body forward and hurls like she's bringing back everything she's consumed in the last seven days. When she eventually stops, she glances up at me with watery, bloodshot eyes.

Even with her messy hair, half of which has escaped from the tie, and the dirty smudge across her cheek and throat left by the filthy asshole, it doesn't distract me from how naturally pretty she is. Even more so than when I last saw her up close when she was fourteen. Although only sixteen and still jailbait, she's already a beautiful young woman.

Fuck. Get your head out of the gutter otherwise, you're no better than the sick bastard that did this to her.

Tentatively, I hold my hand out to her and she takes it as she gets unsteadily to her feet, and fuck, the static electricity that sparks across our palms has me letting go as soon as she's stable. The shirt I gave her is long enough to cover the bottom half of her body, giving her enough coverage for her to pull up her yoga pants. Once her clothes are in place, she stands with her arms wrapped around her waist, her head down. An invisible cloud of shame and embarrassment hangs around her like a shroud, and I can see her visibly turning in on herself. All her previous confidence and swagger seems to have dissipated into thin air. Placing a finger under her chin, I tilt her head up until her face is visible to me. Those sad, teary eyes meet mine and a sharp pain pierces my chest. She looks so lost—so fucking shattered.

"Did he..." I want to ask how far he went. Did the bastard violate her? Did I get there in time? But I struggle to find the right words to string together that won't sound sick and disturbing. "Did he hurt you? Do you need to see a doc?"

Still resting against my fingers, her head rocks from side to side, and when chin starts to drop, I lift it back up. I hold her gaze and wait patiently until she finds her voice.

"I'm okay. He was going to... but he didn't..." An awkward silence falls between us for what can only be a moment, but feels like hours before she adds, "Because you came."

I nod then bend down so I can start to gather the groceries that have spilled from the bag she was carrying.

"The eggs are broken." A sob comes from deep within her and tears pool along the bottom edge of her eyes before they trickle down onto her cheeks. I take the box of broken shells from her and throw them into the dumpster.

I want to bring her into my arms and hold her, make her feel safe, but I know that despite the tears, she's trying to be brave. She is brave. But if I touch her, I'm not sure if it will tip her over the edge and into some kind of crazy.

I do the one thing that I always do in a fucked-up situation. I crack a joke. "Yeah, but the chocolate milk and Hershey bar—" I hold them up so she can see them. "They're still intact, so it could be a lot worse."

She sniggers and a bubble of something not so pretty balloons out of her nose then bursts. She wipes her face with the sleeve of my T-shirt. Nice.

"Is he..." she asks looking over at the shithead that's still laid out.

"He's not dead—just out of it," I answer. At least for now that is. I'd finish the job now if she weren't here to witness it. I watch as she walks over to his motionless body on the floor, swings back her converse covered foot and puts all her power behind the kick that she aims right into his ribs. And fuck, it must have hurt her more than it hurt him, but when she lets out a groan and shakes the pain out from her foot, the look of satisfaction on her face tells me that to her it was worth it.

"Come on, Ninja Girl. Let's get you home."

We could walk the short distance to her house, but I put my helmet onto her head, tapping it down till its firmly in place, and then tighten the strap. I mount my bike before helping her onto the back. Starting her up, I hang the shopping over the handlebar before moving Leah's arms around my waist.

"Hold on tight, Ninja Girl," I shout over the growling noise of the bike. "Don't let go."

I decide to pull up just short of the gate to where she lives so not to advertise our arrival to her ward. I cut the engine, but it takes my gentle untangling of her arms from my waist before she makes any attempt to get off the bike. I stay seated while she stands on the curb side and removes the helmet. I unhook the grocery bag off the handlebars and hold it out to her, but instead of doing a straight swap, she steps forward until she's close enough that I can feel her breath on my face.

Placing the helmet on my head she taps the top, mimicking what I did not moments ago. "Thank you for saving me, Cannon," she says on a breath before grabbing the groceries, turning and running the rest of the way to her front door.

I watch until the door closes behind her and let out a breath, knowing that at least she is now safe in her own home, although maybe not in her head. I punch out a quick text on my phone then start the bike and pull away.

"She remembers me?" I mutter to myself.

As I make my way back to where I found her, my thoughts drift back to the first time I came face-to-face with Leah. Our encounter had lasted a matter of minutes because her brother had ordered her back to her room. The last thing he'd wanted was her getting any unwanted attention from the two dirty bikers that had just dropped by. Yet, even though our paths have only crossed that once, I've watched her many times. She still recognizes me. I won't deny that it shocks the hell out of me, because... why would she?

I arrive just in time; the dirty bastard has come around and is slowly trying to push himself up and off the ground.

"Did you miss me?" I snigger as I walk towards him. His head snaps up at the sound of my voice.

"Oh fuck!" he groans and quickly stumbles to his feet. He sets off down the alleyway, but in his half-bent posture, no doubt from the kick to the ribs from Ninja Girl, and his blood matted left eye from the beating I gave him, he's disoriented. I walk slowly towards him, watching him with a sick sense of pleasure as he slams into the wall a couple of times in his haste to get away. The third time he hits the wall is because of my hands. His shoulders, back and ass slam against the brickwork as does the back of his head when I fist him hard in the face. When I see a flash of black in my peripheral vision I hold back on my next punch and grab him roughly by the shoulder.

"What's your name, fucker?"

"Jared," he mumbles.

"Well, Jared, it's time to take a little trip; my friend here, has organized our ride." I lift his head up by grabbing a clump of his hair so he can see the enormous image of Mammoth coming towards him. He lets out a whimper showing just what a pussy he is. Along for the ride with Mammoth is Mac and Gearhead.

"Mac, take my ride back to the club. You fuck it, then I'll fuck your sister. You get me?"

Mac smirks, nods his head and takes off towards where I left it.

"Gearhead, you take the wheel," I instruct as I start to drag the asshole towards the black unmarked van parked at the entrance to the alley. "We're going to ride in the back so we can point out to Jared here, the error of his ways."

"Preying on young girls"—Mammoth shakes his head—"is a crime in itself, but when you target someone under the protection of the Young Outlaws, then there's only one person that's gonna come out of this scenario totally fucked."

Mammoth pulls open the back door of our 2000 Dodge van and grabs Jared by his throat, lifting him clear off the ground, and launches him into the back. He thuds to the floor, and before he's managed to get on all fours, I'm right beside him giving him a swift kick to the ribs, hopefully in the same spot that my little ninja made impact.

My ninja? What the fuck. She isn't mine. She's just some young chick I'm looking out for to protect the club. Get that shit right out of your head, Colt.

I've always found it strange that everyone calls me Cannon, at least since Mom went anyway. Even my brothers, father and everyone else within or outside the club, but when I talk to myself in my head, I always refer to my given name: Colt. Don't ask me why, I haven't got a fucking clue.

Jared's pussy-ass moaning snaps me out of my contemplation. His pathetic whining grates on every nerve in my body, and I find myself wanting to pull him up onto his feet only to pummel him back into oblivion. However, that would be too quick. I want to make sure he feels every bit of pain that young girl will feel each time her mind is swept back to the moment he grabbed her, put his grubby hands on her and took away her free spirit. Because even if she recovers from this violation, she will always have the mental scar deep within her soul. I just hope she's strong enough to not let it define, control or sully her future. Her past has already given her more heartache than some young girls could take.

I've watched her and, like most teenagers, she's a handful. But this girl? She has an attitude that would make the biggest of bitches on Real Housewives look like the sweet all-American girl from next door. How the hell that old lady puts up with her, I'll never know. From what I've heard, she's one of the IT girls, head cheerleader at school and along with that comes her own little entourage ready to watch her back. However, even though her and her little group of chicks seem to have this authority over most of the girls in school, they don't seem to be your typical mean girls, and I haven't heard any rumors of bullying, which is kind of weird when it comes to the whole popularity scenario. Another thing out of the norm is that she isn't dating any of the football jocks or the basketball, volleyball or track team. That might have something to do with the fact that the Young Outlaws M.C. has made it clear that she's not available, and it's non-negotiable. I sure as fuck ain't giving her brother Jordan any reason to go back on our agreement.

"Brother." Mammoth's deep baritone voice jars me yet again out of my digression. "Are we doing this or what?"

Grabbing Jared by the neck of his T-shirt, I pull him up onto his feet until we're face to face.

"Normally, I would give my victims a choice," I say, my voice eerily calm but laced with venom. "Face, gut or legs... but in your case my friend, it's a given." I smash my fist into his groin with such force that his balls will be now bouncing from his liver to his kidneys like a pinball machine. So, in true game style, seeking maximum points and before the pain gets chance to build to its full momentum, I hit him again, and again, and then once more, because... I want to hit the highest score and... because I fucking can.

Jared's body tries to curl in on itself. It's natural reaction to want to protect, but I continue to hold him up. His legs lift, trying to alleviate the pain, but a swift kick to the kneecap is enough to put a stop to that. I watch as his eyes roll back into his head; his mouth drops open and the words he so desperately wants to hurl in my direction get smothered by the inability to do anything but breath against the pain.

"What's that, Jared?" I act the part, leaning in to hear what he has to say. "Your dick now resembles a pussy seeing that it's now taken up residence inside your gut?" I snigger into his ear. "Well, at least now you've got the right equipment. You even cry like a two-bit, dirty bitch. How sweet that is!"

He takes a couple of sharp intakes of breath, his Adams apple bobbing vigorously at his throat before he finally finds his voice. "Not as sweet as the tears I licked from her face. Just think how incredible the sound of that young little whore's screams would have been with every punishing thrust of my cock as it mutilated her tight little cunt," he grinds out.

The sneer on his face and darkness in his eyes is enough in itself to have me clenching my teeth together so fiercely that they almost crack, but the sickening words induce images in my head of what could have been if I'd not acted like I did; if it had been one of my other brothers watching her; if I hadn't been there for her...

I lose it.

I slam him hard against the inside panel causing the van to rock and veer from side to side until Gearhead gains control. I grab his neck with both hands. My thumbs sit tight under his jaw, fingers and palms wrapped around his throat and with a tight, grip of steel, I squeeze. Watching his face, I take immense pleasure as I see the evil darkness in his eyes ebb away only to be quickly replaced with fear. As he violently begins to struggle, his hands clawing against my hold, his lips turn the colour of slate.

Mammoth puts his hand on my shoulder, but I viciously shrug it off, not saying a word, not trusting myself to speak while the dark and fierce madness controls my brain.

Eyes bulging, blood no longer flowing to Jared's head, his body turns limp.

As I release him, his corpse slumps to the floor. The anger still soars through my veins. Each exhale gushes from my lungs. Every inhale is sucked in with force, until my outrage begins to ebb.

Mammoth moves to my side, crouches down and places his fingers against Jared's pulse point. It's a pointless exercise because I made sure I felt the life drain from Jared's body before I let go.

"Well fuck, brother. I thought we were just going to fuck him up or some shit so he doesn't do it again," Mammoth sighs. "I've never seen you lose it like that before. What the hell did he say to you?"

Ignoring his questioning, I go to the wooden box that's bolted to the floor just behind front passenger seat. Flipping the lid, I grab two large, folded pieces of sacking and throw them at the side of the corpse.

"Cannon, what did he say that got you so riled up?"

"Shut the fuck up, Mammoth. Just leave it will you. Give me a hand bagging the motherfucker up."

By the time we get back to the club house it's dark. On my instruction, Gearhead drives the van around the back of the house, backing it up as near to the swamp as possible without getting it stuck in the long, damp grass.

With the heavily wrapped body slung over his shoulder, Mammoth wades into the swamp up to his knees. The way he flips the weighty sack from him and into the water is effortless, and he quickly retreats to safer ground and away from the gator infested area. We barely get ten feet before we hear the unmistakable sound of splashing as the reptiles take their feed.

CHAPTER FIVE

Leah

I can't stop thinking about him.

When I get home, I stand with my back against the front door for a few minutes while I try to compose myself. It's been a weird and fucked up hell of a day. First of all, while I'd been grabbing my books from my locker, the new guy—who'd just been transferred from Philly—had flirted with me outrageously only to avoid me later like I'd got cooties or Mono or some other infectious disease. On the school bus home, while sitting on the back seat with Reyna and Dana, I'd caught a glimpse of a motorcycle just behind. I'd noticed it because it had those kick-ass, high, silver handlebars. The way they sit on the front of the bike is so hot. It'd reminded me of a porn scene

I'd watched once where a biker dude had a naked girl with her back to the tank, her legs wide open, just like the bars, and his head right between them. The view from the bus window, at that angle... you get what I mean? Dirty, I know, but that's what it had reminded me of.

It's not unusual to see a member of the local M.C on the roads, but what is weird is that every time the bus had stopped to drop-off someone, he'd stopped. Yeah, I know that that's what they have to do—it's the law to not pull around when it stops—but what had been a little freaky was that he'd looked around anywhere and everywhere but at the bus.

When I'd left the bus, I thought he'd gone and that I'd just been paranoid, but then I'd caught sight of him further down the street. I'd been convinced I was being followed. It hadn't been until he'd got off his bike and walked towards one of the houses that I'd let out a sigh of relief. I had laughed so hard at my stupidity because why the hell would anyone be following me?

After dinner, Sheila had planned to walk down to Walgreens for some groceries, but when she'd got up out of the chair, I'd been able to see she was worn out. I guess looking after a teenager isn't easy, and I'll admit I can be difficult at times. She's also getting on a bit. Shit, she's still working, too, even though she's got access to funds to cover the cost of looking after me.

Guilt had me offering to do the grocery run for her. At first, it had been a resounding no, but after promising to stick to the main street and to go straight there and back, she'd conceded. I'd felt euphoric when I'd managed to escape her smothering over protectiveness, albeit for just a short time. I understand it's quite normal for her to be restrictive, especially because she's taking charge of someone else's kid.

I might act like a spoilt brat sometimes, but deep down, I'm grateful as hell to her for the security and love she's shown from the very first day she took me in.

Everything had been going great until I'd made the stupid decision to take a short cut. If I hadn't spent so much time checking out the cosmetics, it wouldn't have even crossed my mind, but I'd taken too long, and I'd just known that Sheila would have started to fret.

The fear had been like nothing else I'd felt before and believe me I've been scared shitless. When my parents died leaving my brother Jordan and me alone, my world had come crashing down. The pain and fear at Jordan's arrest and imprisonment had been all consuming. He'd promised to take care of me, be my protector, but he'd lied. Even my grandma had died, leaving me with no one.

Although the fear from all those monumental occasions in my life had left me ready to pull out my hair, scream till my throat burned, cry till the well was dry, when that man had pushed me against that wall, forced his hand under my clothing, licked the tears from my face, the fear had been so consuming that I'd wanted to die. With every ripping sound of the fabric that covered me, exposing me to the gaze of my attacker, my stomach had rolled, the contents of my last meal threating to regurgitate from my gut. The way he'd run the knuckles at the back of his hand between my legs, I'd thought he was going to put his fingers inside me, but then the sound of his zipper going down had told me that after today, I was never going to be the same again.

Many times I've daydreamed about what it would be like the very first time. I've never envisioned it like that. Not with violence beyond my control—without my consent.

Then it had all stopped.

His hands hadn't been touching me, his body no longer near me, the threat of being violated gone...

All that was left was him: the roughneck of a biker with tattoos, beard and a beanie hat.

The faint but potent smell of leather and grease

had seemed to comfort me when he'd pulled his T-shirt over my head, shrouding me in a veil of protection. His dark eyes had looked at me with concern but without judgement or pity when he'd held out his hand to me, guiding me to his motorcycle.

The parting kick to the asshole's ribs had been necessary: I'd just had to do something to, I don't know, to prove that I'm not so powerless, even though I'd felt so feeble. For a moment, it had made me feel good, but nothing compared to how good it had felt with my arms around the man on the bike: Cannon.

When I shout to Sheila to let her know I am back but desperately needed the bathroom, she doesn't question it, giving me enough time to drop the bag and then slip upstairs to my room.

Stripping out of my clothes, I shove Cannon's T-shirt into my keepsake box at the side of my bed and toss my yoga pants into the laundry basket. Grabbing a clean pair of panties and PJ's, I make a quick visit to the bathroom to wash any visible signs of my encounter off my face and hands, scrubbing at the skin to remove all traces. The need for a shower is almost unbearable, but I know that Sheila will know something is wrong if I take too much time. Looking at my reflection in the mirror, I see my eyes are red rimmed from crying, and I hate myself for being so weak. I quickly pull on my bedwear, press the flush on the toilet and make my way back downstairs.

When I get to the hallway, the shopping bag is gone.

"You forgot the eggs," Sheila laughs as I walk into the kitchen. "And this tin of baked beans is all dinged up."

"I'm sorry. I dropped the bag and they'd run out of eggs."

"No eggs? Hell, what's the world coming to when the grocery store runs out of eggs. Never mind. I can pick some up on Friday when I go to Walmart."

Once she's placed the last item in the cupboard, she turns to face me. "In your PJ's already?"

"Yes, I need to study so I thought I'd at least be comfortable."

"That makes sense. Do you want a drink of cool lemonade hon...?" She stops before she finishes her sentence. "Leah, have you been crying, honey?"

"Aw no, I think it's just allergies. Someone was spraying something on their plants and it kinda misted over in my direction. I'm sure it'll settle down soon."

"Here." She hands me a glass of lemonade. "If it doesn't ease up by the morning, I'll get you something from the pharmacy."

CHAPTER SIX

Leah

One year later

I'm standing at the curbside waiting for the school
bus and it's late. It's my last day of eleventh grade,
and although most of the students are looking
forward to summer break, I'm not. Don't get me
wrong, the first week or two is great: I can stay in bed,
watch some TV, but after that, I'm bored. It drives
me crazy when I hear all the other kids' plans for the
summer break. I'll admit, I'm a little jealous, too.

   I'm especially going to miss my girlfriends, Reyna
and Dana, as both are going away on family vaca-
tions. Reyna is going to The Bahamas—very lush;
Dana is going to Europe, Rome, Italy and then on to

Ireland to visit relatives there. So basically, I'm going to be stuck with nothing to do but help Sheila with any jobs she's wanting to do around the house.

The bus still hasn't arrived and I'm beginning to wonder if it came early. Damn it!

I'd pushed it to the last minute to leave the house and walk down to the pickup point. Sheila had left for work early this morning, so without her usual hollering that it is time to get up that continues until I do, I didn't, which means I had minimal time to pull on some clothes, grab my bag and make it to the bus stop.

Calling a cab to get me to school is out of the question because the four dollars I have in my wallet aren't going to cut it. Even if I start walking now, I'm going to miss registration, which means I'm also going to get slammed with detention.

"DAMN IT!" I curse again.

Walking it is then. Hauling my bag over my shoulder, I'm just about to set off when I hear the deep thumping rumble of a motorcycle. The sound instantly gets my heart racing.

There're a lot of people that say anyone claiming to have a sixth sense are talking total garbage, but I just know it's him—Cannon.

You see, I haven't been able to get him out of my head. He's in my dreams, the first thing that comes to mind when I wake up and the last thing that I think of before I go to sleep. I don't know why because I know I should hate him.

It had been blatantly obvious the first time that I set eyes on him when he turned up at the home I had shared with Jordan with one of the football jocks from school that he and his monster-of-a-sidekick were trouble. I'm damn sure that Jordan had been involved with the Young Outlaws M.C in some way before he was institutionalized.

I haven't seen or heard from Cannon in months, but it will be just my luck, won't it, for him to appear from nowhere when I look like I've just fallen out of bed. Well, I guess I have but that's beside the point. I know I should just keep on walking, eyes forward—then if it is him, he might just ride on by and not notice me—but I can't help it: I need to look. I snap my head to the side, twisting my upper body so I can quickly glance back, and... aww fuck, it's him. I'd recognize that body, his posture, his air of gorgeousness. Not to mention the vivid orange colour of his motorbike.

"Lord, may the ground open up and swallow me whole," I grind out between clenched teeth.

I spin back around to face the way I'm meant to be going, but my bag falls from my shoulder, hitting the floor right in front of my feet. My upper body propels forward, my feet no longer able to go anywhere, and I hit the ground. Pain resonates from my knees up my thighs to my hip, making me squeal out. My hands take the impact, saving my face from hitting the rough surface of the sidewalk causing my skin to instantly burn.

"Motherfucker," I hiss out as the burn turns to a sharp stinging.

"What happened, girl? You lost your ninja powers?" the deep voice just behind me says. I turn my head to face him. The sun behind him gives him a glow like he's some kind of mystical warrior hero.

Why did he have to stop? Couldn't he have just ridden on by instead of stopping to watch my display of utter humiliation? No such fucking luck. And with humiliation comes anger—well it does with me anyway.

"Well are you going to just stand there like a douche or are you going to help me up?" I bark.

Laughing, which only throws fuel onto my annoyance, he grabs me at the waist and physically picks me up and places me back on my feet. As my legs straighten, the skin at my knees pulls tight and the stinging and burning intensifies. I don't have to look down to know that at least two layers of flesh have been skimmed off and that my knees will now resemble raw meat.

"Are you okay?" he asks, taking one of my hands and turning it palm up. He runs a finger across the red, dirty scuff at the base of my thumb and across the lower part of my hand. Even though his fingers look rough and callused, dirt ingrained around the nails and creases of the skin, his touch is soft and gentle.

I take a sharp breath in, and I'm not sure if it's from his touch or fear that he might prod at the sore area.

"You need to clean that up before it gets infected," he adds, pulling up the bottom of his white wifebeater T-shirt to dab at tiny globules of blood. My eyes fall to the now exposed taut skin of his stomach. His jeans hang low, displaying the defined V of his lower stomach. And was that an ab I just saw? Holy shit!

I know he'd taken his T-shirt off when he had given it to me in the alley, but I hadn't been in the right frame of mind to take in the wonder of his finely tuned body. Besides, his cut had hidden most of it. Now, with that little tease, the feeling of disappointment at a missed opportunity has me wanting to reach out and pull his top up further so I can get a better look. I don't though. Instead, I pull my hand away and snap. "What do you think you're doing?"

"Trying to stem the blood."

Now that the sun is no longer behind him, his unearthly glow gone, I can see his face and all his perfect features: dark eyes, strong nose, smooth tanned forehead… His facial hair is thick, almost black, but you can still see his full lips. He has thick eyebrows, the same dark colour as his beard, of which the left one is raised up high on his forehead.

"You should go home and clean up."

"I need to get to school," I huff back. I go to brush down the pleats of my skirt that's are sticking up and are edging on the side of indecent but end up crying out when my grazed palms hit the course wool fabric.

Cannon bends, reaching down, and pulls the hem of the skirt so it sits straight and covers a little more. "Mmm, it's a little short for school isn't it?" he says, still tugging at the bottom.

The knuckles on the back of his hand skim across the bare skin of my thigh and I shiver at the touch.

"Shit, your knees are all scraped up, too."

"Do you mind?" I slap his hand away, purely for appearance purposes, because in reality I want him to touch me more.

"I'm just trying to help." He sighs, holding his hands up in resignation.

"I can take care of myself, thank you very much."

"I think we both know that's not entirely true."

That left eyebrow of his shoots up so high that it nearly disappears under the edge of his hat.

Condescending bastard. And why on earth is he wearing a beanie hat in this weather?

"Well, yes, that was different. I... I. Anyway, I need to get going; I'm already late." Leaning down to grab my bag in haste, I again forget about my damaged hands. This time, I grit my teeth together when the pain hits so the sound that escapes me is a high-pitched cry deep in my throat.

"Give me that," he says, taking hold of the other strap.

"I said I can manage," I reply, pulling the bag towards me. Pain... more pain.

"Let me take it for you."

"I. said. I. can. Manage." Pain. More pain.

The bag goes backwards and forwards a few times as we fight for the win. When I try to hook my arm through the strap, so I don't have to use my hand anymore, it gives him the advantage and he snaps the bag out of my reach.

"Give it back!" I cry, cringing at myself because I sound like a kindergarten rug rat. If it weren't for the height difference, we'd now be face to face.

"Stop being a whiny bitch."

"You stop being a fucking asshole," I retaliate.

"Cut the dirty mouth, Leah; it doesn't suit you,"

he snarls, his voice taking on a darker, more menacing tone. Taking hold of my arm, he walks me over to where he left his motorcycle. Grabbing the helmet that's resting on the seat, he thrusts it towards me. "Put it on; I'll take you to school."

"No, thank you, I can walk."

"Fuck me," he mumbles under his breath. "Should hope so, you do have legs, but if you want to get there in time for registration, I suggest you put on my lid, get your ass on the bike and stop being a prissy little shit."

"I said..."

"LEAH!" he yells.

I want to tell him to go fuck himself, but the look on his face is... well shit!

Begrudgingly, I slam the helmet onto my head and with the force I put behind it, pulling the strap tight, I nearly choke myself. Stomping my foot, arms crossed at my chest, I stand to the side of the bike. I'm waiting for him to get on first, but instead, he picks me up off the ground and dumps me on the back. My skirt flies up, and when I look up to see if he's watching, his eyes are clearly focused right between my legs. The way he's looking at me, heat in his eyes, holy fuck... I feel the blush rising to my face and when he lifts his gaze to meet mine and holds it for what seems like a million minutes, I'm sure I hold my breath for just as many. Abruptly, he turns away, but not before I hear him let out a deep growling sound.

Cannon

Get your fucking head out of the gutter, Colt. You're twenty-six-year-old. She's just seventeen and still in fucking school.

I start up the bike, pull a little too heavy on the throttle and take off at speed. Her body jerks backwards and she holds on tighter. This is torture.

The flash of her white, cotton panties when I'd sat her on the bike had been too fucking much. I'd already been struggling to control my threatening hard on. When I touched her bloody hand, my intention had been to check how hurt she was. It might have been just a graze, but it'd looked sore. To my disgust, my cock had stirred at the contact, and in my head, I'd had to give my junk the hard word, telling it to calm the fuck down. But after I'd got to see the flawless skin of her inner thigh, the edge of her panties, knowing that her tight young pussy was just behind the thin fabric veil, it'd got as hard as stone, pushing against my jeans zipper, desperate to get to her.

Fucking sick bastard.

Again, I'd tried to control my inappropriate sexual urge for her, but when I'd thrown my leg over the bike and got seated, her hands had come around my waist. I'm not a religious guy, but I'd found myself looking up to the sky in hope of some divine intervention.

Give me strength.

She's fucking jailbait, and I've no intention of ending up in a cell after being charged with statutory rape and then targeted by every inmate in the place. I wouldn't blame them either if they beat the living daylights out of me because if the shoe were on the other foot, I'd be fucking up a dirty pedo' too.

I ain't going there. This girl is too young, too pretty for her own good and too much of a fucking dangerous temptation. She's untouchable, so even if she weren't a minor, the risk is way too much. Not just for me, but for the Club.

With the speed I'm going, it isn't long before we're pulling up outside the school. Leah gets off the bike, takes off the helmet and hands it to me. Staying sitting on the bike, I take her bag from between my legs where I've stored it and slip the straps free from the handlebar. I hold it out for her to take, but when she takes hold, I don't release it straight away, keeping her for just a few more minutes.

"Go see the nurse or something. Make sure you get those looked at," I say, pointing to her hands.

"Okay, Dad," she replies with a sarcastic smirk.

I let out a deep sigh, but inside I laugh at the cheek of her. "Stay in school and out of trouble," I add before letting go of the bag.

She turns and starts to walk away.

"And no more short cuts, Ninja Girl," I shout after her. She keeps on walking with her back to me but raises one of her hands, her middle finger standing proud.

I let out a deep laugh and shake my head.

I wait until I see that she's safely inside the building. However, I don't miss the blonde-haired kid who's been eyeing her since she began her walk up the stairs to the swinging doors and who has now slipped into the building right behind her.

My phone starts vibrating in my pocket, so I lean back on the bike and push my hand into my jeans to retrieve it. Creeper's name flashes up on the screen, so I hit the answer button.

Creeper has been a club member for a couple of years and is a creepy fucker, hence the name. He started around the same time as Tag-it and they've hung around together quite a bit. By all accounts when it comes to getting laid, Tag-it loves to share. One on one sex for him isn't enough to sedate his horny ass. But to tag-team a chick with another dude, that's what really gets him off, and Creeper is always happy to oblige. Personally, it isn't my thing. Now... two chicks: been there, done it, got the fucking T-shirt.

"Brother, where the fuck are you?" he asks down the phone.

"Watching the girl."

"Again? Isn't that a job for one of the prospectors, not the V.P?"

"Nothing better to do, and I needed to get away from the club."

"Is that all it is? Seems to me like you've got the urge for some hot, young pussy."

"What the fuck, Creeper. She's just a kid," I hiss out in disgust.

"Yeah, but..."

"No fucking buts, asshole. Don't you even think about going there, do you hear me? I don't want to have to tell you again. Leah is off-limits."

"Ahh, Leah is it now? You can't fool me; you want to fuck her don't yah?"

"Shut the fuck up. Have you forgotten who you're talking to, you shit?" I growl out. Fucker, who does he think he is? "Now did you ring me for something important or just to be an annoying cunt?"

"You need to get your ass back here, pronto. Pres, is on the warpath, asking where the fuck you are."

"Nothing new there," I snicker. "He's nothing but a fucking drama queen." I'm not worried about badmouthing my Pops to the other club members because when it comes down to it, they're just as pissed off with his dramatics and bad decisions as I am. "What is it this time? Bar run out of Jack or something? Whatever it is, get one of the prospectors to sort it out."

"Do you think I would be ringing you if it were that simple?" He gives out a nervous laugh that, over the years I've known him, I've come to realize only happens when this creepy, but otherwise laidback brother, is actually worried about something.

"What's going on?" A feeling of dread washes over me.

"He's called church, and from what I can gather from the call that I overheard him on earlier, our worst nightmare is about to come to fruition."

"Fuck," I gasp out as I slam on my lid. That means only one thing: money. And when it comes to that, Pops is a greedy bastard and will do anything necessary to feed his hunger. "Call Mammoth; tell him to get his ass back. I want one of the prospectors down here at Leah's school now. As soon as he's here, I'll make my way back to the club house."

"Can't you come now? She is in school for fuck's sake."

"Really? So, what if she suddenly decides to cut class, leaves the school and something happens to her?"

"We've got eyes inside the school; we'll get a call if anything does go down."

It's true: we have two kids in there earning a generous sum of cash to keep their eyes and ears open so I'm constantly aware of what is going on while she's out of view. Well, it's not as if the Principle would approve of a couple of hairy bikers hanging around the hallways.

"Look, this is not up for discussion. We have at least one brother watch her twenty-four-seven," I growl. "Got it?"

"Okay, okay," he concedes. "I'll see you when you get—"

I cut the call short because Creeper will certainly be seeing me when I get back, and straight after, he'll be seeing my fist, too, when it comes barreling towards his ugly fucking face.

CHAPTER SEVEN

Leah

It's nine pm in the evening of day two of summer break, and I'm already in my PJ's. Stretched out on my bed, propped up on one elbow and hand resting on my chin, I surf the internet on my cell phone. Even clips of cats and cucumbers on YouTube have become monotonous. Sheila has suggested I spend my time sorting out my room, as it certainly needs decluttering, and that it should keep me busy for at least a couple of days. I must admit, I've still got clothes in my closet that are way too small—shirts too tight across my chest, skirts too short and verging on the line of hooker central—but I hate throwing stuff away. Sheila says that giving it to goodwill isn't throwing it away: it's recycling.

Sighing deeply, I throw my phone on top of my purple quilt and it bounces a couple of times before it comes to rest. I roll over onto my back and stare at the ceiling, wondering how the hell I am going to survive the next eight weeks before school starts again. My phone pings and I'm thankful for the distraction. I open up messenger and the group chat with my two best friends.

DANA: What're my two girls up to?

REYNA: Packing. Do you think I'll have enough with seven bathing suits?

ME: Can you actually die of boredom?

DANA: If not then just skinny dip @Reyna

DANA: I don't know. Have you googled it? @Leah

REYNA: No way. I think I'll pick up an extra one from one of the stores at the airport, just in case. @Dana

REYNA: Scientists have found that those who live tedious lives are twice as likely to die young. @Leah

DANA: God, you're like a walking encyclopedia. You need to loosen up a bit, girl. Let your hair down @Reyna

REYNA: But it goes all frizzy with the

humidity and then just looks like cotton candy.

ME: She was talking metaphorically LOL @Reyna

REYNA: I don't get yah.

DANA: Stop being a goody two shoes. Do something wild. Get out there. @Reyna

ME: Reyna and wild in the same sentence? Wow, that is out there.

REYNA: I'm off to the Bahamas with my parents, not a music festival with a group of college graduates. How wild do you think it's going to get?

DANA: Come on, think of all the beautiful, dark-skinned, sexy toned bodies that will be hanging around on the beach. I bet some of the cabana boys are to die for. @Reyna

REYNA: Did you miss the bit about MY PARENTS WILL BE THERE!

DANA: You need a plan.

REYNA: OMG! Not one of your famous plans. @Dana

Out of the three of us, Dana is the one who comes up with the craziest of ideas. Most of them get stopped before they even get started, but we have a giggle living out the possibilities in our heads. Some of them are outrageous, which is a bit of a surprise because her parents are traditionalist and very strict. Dana handles their prudish rules and restrictions by breaking them any way she can, but she is careful to not get caught so that her sizeable allowance isn't affected. Her parents are loaded, and both are highly regarded within the community. Her dad works for the local government in the planning department, I think. I know he's something to do with construction and permits and that he's very influential in town.

DANA: You go for a swim on your own in your skimpiest bikini and find a hot surfer dude.

REYNA: They do have the perfect climate for surfing in the Bahamas, but I'm not sure if I'm brave enough to go that far out in the water.

DANA: Ok, then someone swimming or paddling, a beach bum… anyone as long as they're hot. Say hi, flirt a little, then the real plan can start.

REYNA: LOL. The real plan? @Dana

DANA: Give your parents the slip. Tell them you're off for a siesta but instead of

going to your room, go meet up with the hottie.

REYNA: I don't think that would be a good idea.

DANA: Why not? Think of the dirty you could get up to in the privacy of his room.

DANA: Stop procrastinating over it @Reyna. Just do it. You keep going on about losing your virginity. Let that hot fucker burst through your hymen like it's the ribbon across a finish line. If you get really lucky, it will be more of a marathon session than a hundred-meter sprint.

REYNA: @Dana stop. I'm not going to just go off with some stranger and you know...

DANA: The word is FUCK, for fuck's sake. Get with the program. Out of the three of us, I'm the only one to have got my pussy pounded, and this would be the perfect opportunity for you. Then we just have to work on Leah.

REYNA: But long-distance relation-ships don't work. Chances are, I wouldn't see them again.

ME: OMG you guys are killing me haa haa ha.

DANA: That's the whole point @Reyna. No commitment, no emotional attachment, no expectations. You get to fuck for fun. Think of it like kindergarten, preschool, whatever you want to call it. It's when you get to spend time finding out what you like and dislike, and the best thing is, you get to decide how long you want to play before the real work starts with all that relationship shit.

REYNA: I just want to lay around and chillax.

DANA: Believe me there's nothing better than an orgasm to help you relax.

ME: Stop! For fuck's sake. You two.

DANA: What? I'm just trying to help.

ME: You two have been driving me crazy for the last three months talking about your vacation plans, and now this? Hot guys, sex in the sun... Just go already. Leave me here to stagnate in peace.

REYNA: I'm sorry @Leah

ME: Ah don't worry. I've got my trusty toys and can always watch naughty step-brother porn once Sheila's out for the count.

DANA: Bah. Bah. Bah. Dana stands tall, wearing a super tight onesie and a bright pink cape. #danatotherescue. #superdana #Iknowwhatyouregoingtodothissummer.

ME: LOL What the fuck? @Dana

DANA: I'm not going.

ME: You serious?

DANA: Yep

REYNA: Oh @Dana, I'm sorry. What happened?

DANA: It's a long story, but to cut a long story short, my parents had a blazing row last night. Mom flat out refuses to go, so the trips off.

REYNA: I'm so sorry.

ME: That sucks big fat hairy balls.

DANA: Yeah but hey! I get to spend the summer with you @Leah. So, what time can you sneak out tonight?

CHAPTER EIGHT

Leah

Usually, Sheila is in bed and snoring like a grizzly bear by nine-thirty, but tonight and totally out of her normal routine, she doesn't retire to her room till after ten o'clock—something to do with one of her programs starting later than normal due to a news flash. It is ten-thirty-six before I hear the steady rhythmic throaty snore from behind her bedroom door. Sheila sleeps like the dead, and I know that even if I had a brass band to celebrate that fact that I can at last leave the house, she still wouldn't wake up before six am in the morning. Since texting Dana to let her know that Sheila has gone to bed, she's been patiently waiting further down the street until I can finally make my escape.

After closing and locking the door behind me, I slip the key into the zip pocket at the front of my bag. Dressed in black yoga pants and hoodie, I sling my small backpack over my shoulder and start a slow jog down the street, but there is no-one around which confuses me. Maybe I'm too late.

Typical.

My phone buzzes in my pocket, so I pull it out.

DANA: Black Toyota Camry, three cars down.

Walking a little further, I spot the car with a very giddy looking Dana sitting in the driver's seat. I let my backpack slide from my shoulder and into my hand, while using the other to open the passenger door.

"Took your time didn't yah?" Dana teases as I slip into the front passenger seat.

She looks absolutely gorgeous and way older than her seventeen years. She's recently had her hair cut in a short crop, with spikey top, and dyed a pretty mermaid shade of green. Not everyone would be able to carry it off, but with her big green eyes, high cheek bones, slightly hooked nose and her bee-sting of a mouth, it works. In total contrast to my clothing, she is dressed in a bright red strapless top that's tight across her chest and matches her lipstick perfectly. She's wearing black shorts that are cut high, and even though she is sitting, I just know that when she stands up, they will barely cover her ass.

She's driving barefoot, but her strappy heels are tucked to one side in the footwell.

"Whose car is this?" I ask once buckled in.

"Ask me no questions and I'll tell you no lies." She smiles big, excitement rolling off her in electrically charged waves.

"Oh fuck! You didn't steal it did you?"

"No," she laughs, the kind that's full of mischief. "After a little manipulation on my part and an enormous amount of guilt on my parents' side, Dad caved and bought me a car."

"This is yours?" I gasp, amazed and slightly jealous of my friend's good fortune. "You lucky bitch."

"I know." She bounces on her seat at the same time as taking the car out of park and pulling onto the road.

"You can drive, can't you?"

"Of course. I've held a learner's permit since I was fifteen," she says matter of fact.

"So have I, but I can't fucking drive." My hands grip a little tighter to the edge of the seat when she takes a left rather sharply.

"Chill, girl. My dad taught me, and I got my full license a month ago. Dad refused to buy me a car at first—said I had to raise the money myself. I think it was his attempt to get me to work for him at weekends, but no way am I going to be his coffee bitch. When the holiday plans came crashing down, well, let's just say I used it to my advantage."

"Why didn't you tell me earlier?"

"Because I wanted to surprise you." She looks over giving me a cheeky wink but then has to pull the car back in line when it starts to drift from her lack of concentration. "Did you bring what I told you to?"

"Yeah, it's in here." I lean forward and pat the top of my backpack that's resting between my feet.

"Okay, jump in the back and get changed."

Crawling into the back of the car, I unzip my backpack and pull out my alternative attire. I peel off my yoga pants, replacing them with bleached denim shorts, skintight like Dana's. The waist sits high with a row of metal buttons as the fly instead of a zip. The fabric is a thinner, softer denim and comes further down the leg, but still high on the thigh. Unzipping my hoodie, I pull it open to reveal a bright yellow sleeveless top. The sheer fabric drapes low at the neckline, showing the soft dome of my breast and the dark fleshy line where they meet in the middle. I pull out my cosmetic bag before shoving my discarded clothing into the top of the backpack.

"So, where are we going?" I ask, brushing a little

bronzer across my cheekbone. I grab hold of the back of the seat in front, my nails digging into the upholstery, while still trying to hold onto the brush and compact, until the car becomes less erratic. I'm not sure whether to talk to her because everytime I do, and she gets distracted. The car swerves and my heart starts to pound. It's like being on a rollercoaster without a restraint.

"You'll see." She answers me through the rearview mirror. I catch sight of her plump red lips puckering and an evil glint in her eye.

"Oh, fuck," I mumble under my breath before I touch the wand of my lip-gloss to my lips. I just know that with Dana involved, it's bound to be something we most certainly shouldn't be doing. Probably a UCF frat party or something like that knowing her. She's always had a thing for older, bad boys.

Undoing the hair tie that's holding my long hair in a loose ball at the nape of my neck, I shake it free. Using my hands, I gently tease my previously curled hair until there's just the right amount falling down my back and over my shoulders. Bending down, I slip on a pair of pale blue wedge sandals; my purple painted toes that match my fingernails peek out of the peep-toe. I hiss from behind my gritted teeth when the straps become problematic to fasten in the confined space.

"Ouch!" I cry out when my head hits the back of the seat at the sudden breaking as we come to a stop.

"Oops, sorry," Dana sniggers, twisting her body around so she can see better into the back seat. "You look fooking hot babe, but you need just one tiny adjustment." Crawling into the back to join me, she stands, but yet crouches over me and starts to roll up the legs of my shorts, until they're much higher up my thigh, meaning much further up my ass. "Now that is savage."

"Thanks," I laugh as she crawls back into the front seat. Pushing open the driver door, she snatches her shoes from the footwell and steps out of the car.

"Where are we exactly?" I question. It's dark out apart from the shards of moonlight breaking through the gaps in the tall trees. In fact, all I can see are trees. No houses, no buildings, nothing.

"Come on!" she shouts, banging on the roof of the car.

Stepping out, my feet hit rough ground, and I'm not ashamed to say, I'm wondering, what the fuck.

"What the fuck, Dana? Why are we in the middle of nowhere?"

"Tru...ust me," she stutters, trying not to lose her balance while putting on her heels. "We're going to leave the car here and walk the rest of the way. Don't worry, it's not far now."

"Shit," I grumble when I go over on my ankle. "Damn-it, Dana, if I'd known we were going hiking, I'd have brought suitable footwear."

"Leah, shut-up will you. I'm in heels, too. You'll thank me once we get there."

"This better be good," I huff out.

"Oh, believe me, this is more than good: this is going to be the best night of your life."

CHAPTER NINE

Leah

After walking, or should I say stumbling, for another ten or fifteen minutes, the tree line opens up as well as the dirt track, and right in front of us is a large, aging, two-story house. If it weren't for the music that is getting louder, the nearer we get, and the people milling around outside on the huge porch, I'd be thinking that we've just walked into a hammer house of horror movie.

At one side of the house is a black van; to the other is a large outbuilding with a dozen or more motorcycle's parked in front. The only light against the dark vehicles is when the moonlight reflects off the shiny chrome handlebars.

A fire pit sits at the front of the house. What

looks like upturned crates, boxes and such are placed around it where people sit, laughing and drinking. When the smoke wafts in our direction, the pungent smell of pot has me stopping in my tracks.

"What's going on, Dana?"

She stops and turns towards me. "It's a house party."

"Who does this house belong to, Dana?" I ask already suspecting what the answer will be.

"Just, a club..."

"What club, Dana?" I hiss.

"Erm, the Young Outlaws."

"What the fuck, Dana! We can't do this."

"Why not?"

"Because... because..." Fuck! What if Cannon is in there? What the hell will I do? Excitement at the prospect of seeing him has my stomach in knots, but however much I'd love to see the look on his face, seeing me here dressed, well, kind of slutty, I'm pretty sure that this is a bad idea. "We need to go back to the car, like now." I tug on Dana's arm, but she's not going anywhere.

"Hey, ladies. What are you doing hanging around in the woods at night?" A deep voice rumbled from out of nowhere.

"Oops, too late," Dana gives me a fake smile before grabbing my hand and dragging me towards the leather-clad biker. The guy is tall and lanky. A thick head of curls sits on top of his head. It's long and unruly and hangs just past his chin. His jaw line is short and narrow, but it may be his long, pointed messy beard that extenuates it. A cigarette hangs loosely from his lips, the pungent smell drifting over to us telling me that it's not a regular smoke. His baggy jeans sit extremely low on his hips, blue T-shirt that's a little short on his upper body barely covering his stomach. I'm sure that with the slightest lift of his arms, and it if it wasn't as dark as it is, I'd see the top of where his pubic hair begins. Unless he is shaved of course, but I doubt it by the look of his general grooming. His leather cut hangs loosely; the word prospector lay across one side of his chest.

"Do you know that you're on private property?"

"Sorry, we'll just go," I say nervously. "Dana," I hiss, while tugging on her arms, pulling her back towards the direction from which we came. But she doesn't move, her feet firmly rooted to the spot. An uneasy feeling rumbles in my stomach, threatening to purge this evening's dinner.

"We heard you were having a party and well..." Dana purrs in her best sex voice. "We were actually wondering if we could join in?" She moves a little closer to the prospector, sashaying her hips like she's making her way towards a stripper pole and about to put on a very provocative show.

A smile slashes across the Prospectors face as his eye's skim over her from head to toe, giving extra time and perusal to her tits, hips and her long, slender legs.

He pauses for a moment as if considering his options. "You girls look a little young to be out so late at night, never mind wanting to party with a load of biker dudes. Things can get a little... rough around here. Maybe you should just run along home."

"We're old enough and know what goes on here," she replies, putting on her best husky voice.

"You have no fucking idea," he chuckles, shaking his head.

As I walk up to stand beside her, my intention to convince her to leave, I watch in awe as I see her slip her finger between her bright red lips and suck on it seductively.

"Aww, come on now. Let us have some fun with you," she mumbles while letting her tongue run rings around her finger before sucking the whole thing deep into her mouth and then pulling it out with a pop.

Fuck. This poor guy has no chance of refusing her now. She looks as sexy as hell and even I am feeling the undeniable tingle of arousal in the pit of my stomach.

"Fuck, girl, I ain't going to turn you away, but don't say I didn't give you the chance to walk." He steps up to her. "People around here call me Toothpick, so what's your name, sugar?" He drapes his arm around her shoulders and starts walking her towards the house.

"I'm Carrie," she lies. "Are you coming, Patti?" she asks, winking at me over her shoulder.

Fucking Patti? Isn't that the name of one of Marge's sisters in the Simpsons? I'm going to kill her later.

I follow them because, what choice do I have? The nearer we get to the house, the more visible the state of ill-repair that it's in becomes. The whole place looks shabby, dark and unloved, but then again, it's a motorcycle club, so it wasn't ever going to be the Hilton was it?

As we step onto the porch, we're met with what must be one of the club whores writhing on the lap of a huge, familiar looking monster of a man with a thick beard and wearing a bandana. I know I should avert my eyes, but I'm mesmerized by the way he's flicking between chugging down a beer and taking a deep draw of a fat cigar, but at the same time is seemingly unaffected by the fact the girl is riding him hard and is groaning and whimpering like she's seconds away from orgasmic lift-off. He is apparently getting no sexual gratification from it himself.

I'm not a total prude: I've watched porn, but it being right in your face, in real life... well, I honestly don't know where to look.

Walking through the door, we're led into a large room with a few scattered couches and chairs in it. A couple of low tables sit in between, overflowing with beer bottles, glasses and ashtrays full to the brim with ash and cigarette ends. Although, the pungent smell that's lingering in the air suggests it's not standard tobacco smell that's attacking my nostrils. It's weed, sweat and sex.

Two guys wearing cuts are drinking and laughing while playing pool at the table over to the right side of the room. To the left is a solid, dark wood bar that's decorated with Harley signs and various other biker paraphernalia. As we walk towards the bar, a young guy—I assume the one who is attending it—stands at the other side, leaning against it wiping a glass. He has a salacious smirk on his face as he watches a guy with his head under the skirt and firmly between the legs of a woman who is sitting on the edge of the bar. Her head is tipped back, her mouth open, as she moans out in pleasure. It's clear exactly where his mouth is and what it's doing.

"What's your poison, girls?" Toothpick asks us, oblivious to what's going on right next to us suggesting it's a common occurrence here. I, on the other hand, barely register Dana's response to Toothpick's question as she answers for us both. I'm dumbstruck. I know I should turn away, but I'm unable to take my eyes off the woman who has become increasingly noisy as she gets nearer to her release.

I am shocked at the way it is affecting me. I can't see what the guy is doing to her, but I damn well know that he must be talented with his tongue. That is enough to have my body humming and heat pooling between my legs. Holy shit. I'm so turned on that my panties are wet, and my hard nipples are pushing against the fabric of my bra.

Just as the woman screams out some undecipherable babble, Dana thrusts a bottle of beer into my hand and gains my attention.

"Kinky voyeur," she laughs. "Come on. Drink. Let's get hammered." Placing the bottle to her lips she knocks it back and doesn't come up for a breath until she's chugged half of it down.

"Fuck me," Toothpick gasps, well impressed at Dana's drinking skill.

"Only if you can perform like that guy can," she laughs, pointing over my shoulder.

I turn just in time to see the guy lift his head from

underneath the fabric. He swivels his head in our direction, his mouth still slick with the evidence of his sexual prowess. When our eyes meet, the smile of satisfaction on his face slips instantly and is replaced with a look of thunder. We look at each other, neither of us expecting to come face-to-face, especially in these circumstances. I'd thought I might catch a glimpse of him hanging around, but the last thing I'd been expecting was to find him with his head between some club whore's legs.

"What the fuck?" He hollers, wiping his mouth with the hem of his T-shirt.

"Hey, V.P. This is Carrie and Pattie; they just wanna drink, maybe have a bit of fun," Toothpick winks, looking all proud of himself.

"I don't fucking think so," Cannon grits out. He grabs hold of my forearm and starts pulling me towards the door.

"Dana?" I shout over my shoulder while trying to get free of Cannon's grip. "Let go of me, asshole."

"Dana? I thought you said your name was Carrie," Toothpick grumbles, taking Dana by the arm and marching her out right behind us.

I can hear Dana trying her best to sweet talk Toothpick behind me, but I'm distracted by the electrical charge that seems to be coursing through my body from Cannon's firm hold on me—along with the embarrassment of being hauled out of the place and passing a group of laughing, jeering douchebags.

"Brother?" the bearded monster shouts as we walk down the steps at the front of the house.

I turn to see him quickly rise from the chair he's been sitting on, unceremoniously pushing the girl still mounted on his dick to one side so she falls to the floor. It happens quickly, but I still get a quick flash of his erect dick before he tries to squash it back into his pants. From his pained expression, I don't think it's an easy feat.

"Not now, Mammoth!" Cannon roars. Ah, that's why he's familiar to me: he'd been with Cannon when he turned up to the house years ago to see Jordan.

Cannon stops suddenly and turns towards him. "Keys," he barks, holding up his hand. Mammoth throws him a bunch of them, and he catches it with his free hand.

"You need any help, brother?" Mammoth asks as we resume our walk.

"Nope, I got this."

We come to a stop next to a black Ford truck. Swinging the door open, he pushes me towards it. "Get in."

I don't argue because the tone of his voice is downright frightening.

Once seated he slams the door shut just before the locks click into place, trapping me inside.

"Bastard," I scream, banging on the window and feeling a little braver now that I have the barrier of the metal between us.

He casts me a 'don't fuck with me' look over his shoulder before he storms over to Toothpick and Dana, who are now standing next to Mammoth.

CHAPTER TEN

Cannon

Today has been a total mind fuck.

After yet another volatile argument with Pops about working with the Mexican traffickers, to the point where it took both Mammoth and Gearhead to pull me off the fucker, now this.

"How did you get here?" I ask Leah's friend.

"Car of course," she replies cockily.

"What fucking car?" I'd already looked around, and all the cars that were here were cars that I recognized as belonging to members or the club.

"It's parked over there somewhere." She waves her hand in a general direction. I'm guessing she's left it on the dirt track, just about a quarter mile away and only accessible by cutting across the rough ground.

"Brother." I direct my words to Mammoth. "Take her back to her car and make sure she heads off home." I step up to her, getting all in her face. "Don't fucking come around here again, you hear me? Because if you do, I'll make sure every one of my guys gets to take their turn, till you're well and truly fucked. You get me?"

"Yes," she murmurs, and fuck if her pupils don't blow with the thought of that. Shit, she's a dirty little bitch.

"Fucking get her out of here Mammoth before I throw her to the wolves."

As soon as I know Leah's friend is out of ear shot, I turn towards Toothpick. Placing my hand on his shoulder, I pull back my fist and smash it into his stomach. He drops like a ton of lead, knees hitting the ground, groaning like I've just pulled his left testicle off with a pair of pliers.

"What the fuck V.P," he whines.

I grab his shoulder and pull him to his feet before wrapping my hand around his throat. "You were told that she was off limits, so why the fuck would you think that it was acceptable to let her be here?"

"Who? I don't know what... Oh shit, that's Leah

Sparks, the girl we're meant to be watching? Fuck, I didn't know."

"Not good enough," I sneered. I'm just about to plant my fist in his face, when hands grab hold of my raised arm, holding it back. I turn to find Conda standing behind me.

"Cannon, come on, man. He couldn't have known who she was. He's a dumb prospect and only just patched over from Cherrywood. Shit, he still doesn't know where to go to take a piss. Come on, brother, let him go."

"So, how the fuck did she even get here? Who's meant to be on watch?"

"JB."

"Fucking, Johny Bravo. He'll be sniffing around some gash rather than doing his fucking job." Because that's what JB does. He's a pretty boy who uses more hair products in a day, than the local hair salon does in a month. He also has an uncontrollable need to impress the ladies.

"Leave it with me. I'll find out where the fuck he is and give him a fucking for it. In the meantime, I think you better go see to her"—he points towards the truck— "before she causes any damage."

I turn to find Leah with her legs up, both her bare feet flat against the windscreen. Her face screwed up in concentration, the tip of her tongue jutting out of her mouth as she puts all her effort into kicking out the glass. With each impact, her expression changes to a grimace from the pain that must be vibrating up her legs to her hips.

"For fuck's sake," I rasp, running my hand over my short-cropped hair. Walking back to my truck, I go straight to the driver's side and pull open the door.

"Cut it out!" I shout at her as I jump in.

Totally ignoring me, she continues to beat her feet against the window.

"Leah. Stop." I lean over the center console and grab both her legs just above the ankle and pull them, her body turns in the seat until her feet are in my lap. "You're going to fucking break something."

"Aw diddums. Worried I'll damage your precious truck?" She tries to swing her legs back to have another go, but I tighten my grip.

"I was referring to your legs, Leah. You're going to crack a bone or something if you keep it up, so fucking stop."

She huffs out. Her body relaxes a little, but her arms are crossed in front of her, a scowl on her face.

She's a stubborn, feisty fucker that's for sure, but for some reason I find it kinda cute. She has this built in resilience and fight in her that astounds me and pisses me off all at the same time. After staring me out for a few minutes, she turns her head and looks out of the windscreen that thankfully is still in one piece. I look down at her feet that are still resting in my lap: narrow with delicate toes, the nails painted a shiny purple. My eyes rake up past her slim ankles, over her firm calves to her slender thighs stopping at the edge of her faded blue shorts. The fabric has ridden up high between her legs, and I can see the edge of her yellow panties. I know I shouldn't be looking, so I avert my eyes but only as far as to the metal buttons at the front of her shorts. She has full curvy hips that I know have a fine ass connected to them that sweeps into a tight, slim waist. The yellow top hangs low at the front giving me a glimpse of the bra that matches the panties. Fuck! The valley between her tits is spectacular, and I can only imagine how good it would feel to let my tongue slip between the plump flesh.

"Shit," I mumble under my breath when I look up to find her watching me eye fucking her. "Put your seatbelt on!" I bark at her, roughly pushing her legs back over to her side. Firing up the truck, I keep my eyes fixed forward, but I can feel the waves of defiance rolling off her. I'm in no doubt that she'll be giving me the stink eye. Out of the corner of my eye I see her reach for the clip, pull the strap over her body and fix it into the buckle.

The wheels spin on the loose gravel, and dust

plumes up around us as I take off at speed down the dry dirt track toward the main road. Only the rumbling of the engine and the hum of the aircon can be heard in the cab. The silence between us gives clearance for my mind to mull over the night's events which in turn fuels my internal turmoil.

What the hell had she been doing at the club? Why the hell hadn't someone recognized her and sent her packing? Fuck, I know what goes on and can only imagine what she's seen. The last thing I'd been expecting to see when I came up from underneath's Nail's skirt was her. The only reason I'd given the impromptu display out front and not in the privacy of my room, was because of my father's constant digs that I should get more pussy.

The relationship with my father has become ever more strained. Not just because of this Mexican shit-storm. He's a constant pain in the ass, picking fault with everything I do, dragging me back to the club house for shit that one of the prospects could easily handle. Then the next minute, I'm sent out to do a major deal with the Chinese while he sits on his lazy ass, snorting shit up his nose and having one of the whores bounce on his wrinkly old cock. Luckily, the people I do deal with respect me and hold me in high regard, if not higher than they do my father. Over the years, he's played some dirty tricks that could have brought the club to its knees. If it hadn't been for Mammoth and me smoothing over some shitty situations, then every one of us would be either dead and buried under a ton of dirt, or alligators' fodder.

My fucking father. He's nothing but a bastard, constantly trying to push me into submitting to his ideas—ideas that I know are wrong for the club. If my older brother had stuck around, would things be different? Who knows? But for now, he's still the president of the club and still my Pops.

The switch of thought has temporarily distracted me from the problem I have sitting right next to me, but at least my temper has ebbed somewhat.

"What the fuck were you doing at the club?" I ask, breaking the silence. She doesn't respond, just keeps her arms crossed, head turned to the side window looking out into the darkness. "It's not the type of place you should be hanging out."

"Well excuse me." She swings her head around to face me. "Since when has it been any of your business what I do?"

"You're too young to be around that shit, Leah."

"I'm seventeen. I can look after myself."

"Really?" I gasp out a laugh. "You're fucking shitting me. Have you forgotten what happened last year?"

"Really?" she mimics back. "You're fucking shitting me? That's not something you forget easily." She pauses, takes a shuddering breath as if holding back her frustration. "But I sure as hell don't need you butting in like some overzealous Neanderthal, dragging me out of there. That was so humiliating."

"Tell me, Ninja Girl, seeing as you're all grown up now, what exactly were you planning on doing at the club house?

"Have some fun, but you put a stop to that, didn't you?"

"So, you're telling me if one of the guys had picked you up, laid you on the pool table and..."

"Licked my pussy?" she interrupts.

"Shit!" I curse out, swiping my hand down my face at her glaring referral at catching me in a compromising position. I take my eyes off the road for a moment and quickly glance at her.

"You're a fucking joke, seeing as you had your head stuck between that dirty whore's legs," she scoffs. "You're just a two-faced, hypocritical motherfucker."

"Watch your mouth," I growl back at her. The image of her laid out on the blue felt surface flashes through my mind. The Young Outlaws Club wording slashed across the cut that covers the broad back of the guy holding her legs apart... It's not me, it can't be me, but the thought of it being some other club member, or anyone else for that matter, is enough to fuel my simmering temper, bringing it to boiling point.

I'm so fucking mad. The urge to grab someone by the throat, anyone but her, to vent my anger is all consuming. Instead, I tighten my grip around the steering wheel until the skin around my knuckles is white. I put my foot down heavy on the gas, the powerful engine of the truck giving no resistance as I take it well over the speed limit. Out of the corner of my eye I see her stiffen, her hands clasping onto the seatbelt that's tight across her chest.

What the fuck am I doing? I mentally kick myself, talking myself down off the ledge until my temper begins to level out and I ease off the gas, letting the truck come back to a reasonable speed. The last thing I want to do is scare her, although the idea of throwing her over my knee and slapping the hell out of her ass for being a sassy little bitch, for being so stupid and putting herself at risk is tempting, but it would only fuel my inappropriate thoughts.

"Why'd you come here Leah?"

She opens her mouth to speak but before she does, I say sternly. "The truth, Leah."

Her face is like thunder, but as I look at her, my eyebrows raised in question, the storm depicted in her face begins to ebb. Her gaze drops to her hands that are now resting in her lap, her shoulders fall as if in defeat, and she shifts uncomfortably in her seat, but still doesn't speak.

"Leah, do you realize what danger you put yourself in tonight? Being out this late, just you two girls? It's fucking risky, Leah and the club isn't the type of place for you, nor does it hold the kind of people that you should be hanging out with."

"Yet here I am, hanging out with you," she snarks, kicking the side panel of the truck.

"Leah!" I shout, grabbing her arm and giving it a quick jerk. "Quit fucking kicking, will yah?"

"Then stop treating me like a child."

"Not while you're acting like one," I growl back at her, letting go of her. "What goes on there is not for you—not now, not ever. You understand me?"

She doesn't reply, but the sound of her rapid breathing has me glancing over to her. Her mouth is tightly clamped shut, her normally fleshy lips pursed into a thin line. A pink flush to her cheeks tells me she's well pissed. With every deep, rapid breath she takes in her frustration has her breasts bouncing in the tight-fitting top she's wearing, her nipples clearly outlined against the fabric. When she shivers, I realize the temperature of the cab is chilly and that she must be feeling it in her tiny shorts and thin top. I reach behind the seat and pull out a spare checked flannel shirt that I keep there for emergencies.

"Here." I hold the garment out to her."

"I'm fine," she snarks back at me, but her body shudders again, giving away the truth of the matter.

"Leah, for fuck's sake, you're cold. Just take the fucking thing." When she still doesn't take it from me, I drop it into her lap.

Thank fuck the road is deserted because my concentration constantly flicks back and forth between the road and her. I can't seem to stop looking at her with her azure blue eyes, silky blonde hair and soft pink lips. Her skin has a deep honey tone to it from where the sun has kissed it, every visible inch flawless and finished off with splattering of freckles across her petite nose. She's stunning and too fucking sexy for her age and her own good, yet she seems to be totally unaware of the undeniable sexual aura that emanates from her.

With a loud huff, she shakes out the garment but instead of putting it on, she just lays it over the front of her upper body and arms, right up to her chin like a blanket. Pushing up the fabric with her hand that's underneath she brings it to her nose and sniffs it.

She's so fucking cute.

"You might think I'm just an overzealous Neanderthal," I say in a softer, more level tone, "but it's only because I don't want anything to happen to you. There's a lot of fucking assholes out there Leah, people who are just waiting to take advantage of a pretty girl like you." I don't mention the sick bastards who could snatch her off the streets and over the Mexican border, drugged up and sucking dick for a few pesos—the same sick bastards that my father is all too eager to work with.

I feel her gaze on me and it takes all my resolve not to turn my head and let myself get lost in the blue of her eyes.

CHAPTER ELEVEN

Leah

The conversation may have come to an abrupt halt, but the questions bounce around in my head at light speed.

Why does he even care?

Why would I be of any concern to him? In his eyes I'm just an annoying kid that seems to turn up every now and then like a bad penny.

He thinks I'm pretty.

"Where are you taking me?" I ask him, still reeling from the good cop / bad cop scenario that he's been playing. One minute he's growling like a bear with a stick up his ass, then the next minute he's all mother hen, like he cares about me. Talk about mixed signals; it's a complete and utter mindfuck.

"Home," he replies softly, then adds more sternly. "Exactly where you should be."

"Jesus Christ," I murmur under my breath.

"What?" he growls back, proving my early conjecture. "Where do you think I was going to take you at this time of night?"

"I don't know, church maybe—get me to renounce all my sins. Not that I personally think wanting to have a bit of fun for a change comes under the category of sin. Or maybe it's you that feels the need to repent?"

"Believe me, Ninja Girl, I'm way past that, and if I did indeed want to seek forgiveness then I'd need to go to the Vatican itself, kiss the feet of the Pope and the ass of a thousand Cardinals before they'd even consider it."

I can't help but snigger at his response but then stop abruptly when for the first time, it truly hits me who he is. He wears the 1%er badge, so it's blatantly obvious that he's a law breaker. I guess the Club name gives it away. I wonder to what extent his unlawful acts pertain: drugs, guns, who knows... I've watched The Sons, but those television programs are dramatized to make them more desirable to the mass market. Aren't they? I'm sure there could be an element of truth to them but not to the extent of dead bodies in unmarked graves, gun wars and retribution.

It had been like a kick to the gut when I'd seen Cannon's face appear from between that woman's legs, but when he'd gone all protective, marching me out of the club house, it'd had my heart pounding and my body alight with excitement.

I can't dispute the clear signs telling me that I should keep away from him—that he's trouble—but I also can't deny the fact that when I'm with him, he makes me feel safe and I haven't felt this since my brother Jordan left. But why does he act this way, giving me the impression that he cares? Why on earth would he give any fucks about me?"

"Why do you even care?" I blurt out aloud my questionable thoughts just as he pulls his truck up outside my house.

"Go inside, Leah. Go get some sleep."

"Shit!" I curse out as a feeling of dread bubbles up from my stomach and into my chest when my stupidity hits me. I've been so angry that it hadn't even crossed my mind.

"What's up?" he turns towards me, as I fidget in my seat.

"My key: it's in the pocket of my backpack and I've left it in Dana's car. I can't get in," I choke out. "What am I going to do?"

"Knock on the door like any normal person would do?"

"I can't. Sheila doesn't even know that I snuck out. If she finds out, she'll go apeshit."

"Then I guess you're going to have to face the consequences. Maybe she'll ground you and give me a break."

"What?" I look at him confused. "A break from what?"

"Having the misfortune of coming across you when all you seem to do is cause havoc. If you're at home, surely you can't get into any trouble or turn up at my club house."

I sit rigid in my seat, gripping the sides, not knowing what to do. If I wake up Sheila, she'll interrogate me until she finds out exactly what I've been up to tonight, and that would simply trigger full blown Armageddon. My recently gained, albeit minimal, freedom and decrease in her overbearing protectiveness would be lost, and my dream of going to an out-of-state college would be just that: a dream.

I turn to him, pleading with my eyes, begging for him not to make me do this.

"For fuck's sake," he gripes, looking upwards to the interior of the cab roof as if hoping that it might offer a solution to my predicament and hissing. "You, Ninja Girl, are going to be the death of me."

Pushing his door open, he jumps out, quietly

closing the door behind him. He stops and reaches into the bed of the truck, before walking around and opening the door at my side. His face is like thunder, his eyebrows all hunched up in a deep scowl line across his forehead. He's really pissed.

"Come on," he says quietly, but the harshness in his voice only confirms just how fucking mad he is. I get out of the cab, and when he takes my hand, an instant tingling sensation shimmies to my fingertips, across my palm and up my arm before dancing its way around the rest of my body.

Instead of leading me up to the front of the house, he leads me down the side and around to the back door. It's dark at the back of the house with no security lighting to illuminate our way, but the moon is full, giving us just enough visibility to ensure that we don't end up on our asses. We arrive at the back door, and he lets go of my hand. It's then that I see he's holding a black roll of fabric in his other hand, which is what he must have grabbed from the back of the truck.

"Hold your hand out flat," he instructs, turning it palm up. "Both of them," he adds before untying the boot lace that is wrapped around the fabric roll. Once it's free, he unravels the fabric across my hand to reveal a row of various slim metal tools with different edges and shaped tips, some of which are bent at the end like a Hex Key. Taking out one with a bent end, he slots it into the bottom of the lock where the key would fit. Sliding out one of the narrow tools that looks like a very thin blade with a serrated edge, he places that into the top part of the lock. While twisting the Hex key side to side, he quickly pumps the serrated blade in and out at the same time. Within a matter of seconds there's a click and the lock releases. Slowly, he pushes the door open, takes the roll out of my hands and thumbs at me to go inside.

Before I step inside, I turn to face him and find him standing so close that our bodies are nearly touching. My hands fidget nervously in front of me, but when I feel my knuckles brush across the fabric of his jeans, I quickly snatch them away flinging them behind my back.

Oh my God. Did I just stroke his junk?

My tongue instinctively flicks out to wet my dry lips, heat spreading across my face. I can only hope he doesn't notice in the dim light but when I see the intensity in his eyes, I blush even more, knowing that he felt my unintentional touch.

"I, umm." Words get stuck between my brain and my mouth, refusing to break out.

I don't think it possible for us to get any closer,

but when he takes another step towards me and leans into me, his hard chest pressing against my boobs, I know I am wrong. The heat of his breath caresses the side of my face, his lips so close. My heartbeat races, and my body hums. The pulse between my legs is ticking like a bomb waiting to explode, waiting for him to make his move—for his wet mouth to make final contact with my heated flesh. All I would need to do is move my head to the side, and our lips would meet.

"Leah," he growls seductively. His mouth now next to my ear, the side of his face resting against mine the tension palpable between the two of us. He's hot, so fucking hot, and he's right next to me. Oh, my word. I want to get down and dirty with him —let him do the kind of things to me that I've seen on screen but not experienced... but all that disperses quickly with his next words.

"Graduate school, go to college and stay out of fucking trouble. Do you hear me? Because I won't be around to save your ass. Now, go to bed." Stepping back from me, he takes hold of my shoulders and spins me around until I'm facing into the house. With a gentle push until I'm far enough into the house, he pulls the door shut behind me. A click tells me the latch is secure.

Turning back to the door, I see the shadow of his

huge frame disappear. He's gone. Disappointment, annoyance and an equal amount of humiliation hits me hard and before I know it, I have tears of rage running down my face.

CHAPTER TWELVE

Leah

"Asshole," I hiss under my breath. "Fucking asshole. I hate you Cannon... whatever the fuck your name is. You're a dick, a frustrating douchbag of a cock, and I detest you. Dick, dick, dick." I continue to mutter as I stumble with tear-induced, distorted vision through the darkened hallway. My intention is to make my way quietly to my room, but as my foot hits the first step I'm temporary blinded by the brightness of the overhead light.

"Where the hell have you been?" Sheila's voice rings out. "And what the hell are you wearing?" The harshness in her voice is clearly fueled by fear and relief. She stands firm, fisted hands resting on her hips, creases of pain and disappointment etched on her face and tangible in her eyes.

"I just..."

"Don't lie to me, Leah. I heard the truck pull up. When I looked out of the window, the last person I expected to see was you and one of those bikers sneaking around outside. As far as I was aware, you were safely tucked up in bed." Walking past me, she goes to the back door and checks the locks. "Thank goodness it's not damaged."

"If you knew it was me outside, then why didn't you unlock the door?"

"By the time I realized you didn't have your key and had got mine from my purse, your outlaw buddy had flipped the lock. Never mind that: don't you dare try and deflect my question. I'm not the one who's been out God knows where until the early hours of the morning."

I check my watch. Shit, I hadn't realized it was so late.

"Do you realize that what this... this... man has done is breaking and entering? I need to report this."

"No, no," I beg going to her side. "Don't."

"Give me one good reason why I shouldn't call the police."

For some unfathomable reason, I feel I need to protect him. The last thing he needs is for the cops to get involved, especially with the club. Surely I owe him that much, at least.

"It wasn't his fault: I asked him to. Please, Sheila."

"If you tell me exactly what you've been up to tonight—and I mean the truth, Leah… all of it—then I'll consider not going to the police with this."

"Okay, okay. Dana picked me up in her car and we went for a drive."

"Dana has a car—has she even got her license?"

"Yes, she just got it. Anyway, we took a wrong turn and…"

"Woah, stop. Coffee, I need coffee."

"I'll make it," I offered.

"Too right you will." She waves me towards the kettle before taking a seat at the counter.

After I make the hot drink, I sit beside her and tell her my version of the events. I miss out the fact it had been Dana's idea to go to the Young Outlaws MC club house by making out that we took a wrong turn. The last thing I want is for her to put a ban on me seeing her, so I have to make sure it looks like it was just an unfortunate miscalculation and lack of road knowledge. I also cut out the details of the debauchery that I'd been visually exposed to while I was there. In fact, I don't even mention that we had entered the actual club house, only that we had stumbled across the building. I did however tell her the truth about Cannon. Well, only the part about how he had made sure that both Dana and I had got home safely and away from any undesirable attention of any of the bikers. I didn't mention the fact our initial encounter was him with his head between a club whore's legs, giving her an alternative kind of lip service.

Once I explain that I'd stupidly left my key in Dana's car and that was why Cannon had worked the lock, her face begins to soften somewhat.

"Why were you crying when I found you in the hallway?"

Oh shit. How do I explain this one? I can hardly say it was due to the fact I'd been desperately hoping for Cannon to make a move on me, and that my tears were purely out of frustration that he hadn't. That won't go down well. But hell, I tell her anyway because now that I think about it more rationally, he would have been wrong to do so. I might think I'm a young woman in my head, but the law has a totally different take on the matter, seeing as I'm still under the legal age to have sex with someone of his age.

"So, if you think about it, he didn't do anything wrong." I plead with my eyes, because however much I hate him, I don't want him to get into trouble with the cops. I still owe him for saving me all those years ago. I hope this is enough to convince her because the last thing I want to do is bring up that particular horror story.

"Who'd have guessed?" she chuckles softly. "A gentleman in a cut."

"I think that's going a bit far," I say, shaking my head.

"Leah, stop while you're ahead," Sheila rebukes. "When I saw you crying, I thought that he'd done something... unthinkable to you. I might have come across angry, but I was worried sick."

"Sheila, I'm fine. Honestly."

"Well, don't ever do anything like that again, do you hear me?" she warns. "You're grounded."

"Till when?" I cry.

"I don't know. I haven't decided yet. Now go to bed before I put you to work, because believe me young lady, I've got a list of chores with your name on it. Now shoo."

Shit. Summer break is not going to be fun. Roll on next semester.

CHAPTER THIRTEEN

Cannon

The following year

Bang, bang, bang. The head of the bed crashes against the wall with every violent thrust I make. My hand slaps again, the firm young ass already showing signs of my spanking. Running my palm across the reddened cheeks, I feel the heat of her skin as I sooth them with my gentle touch. I grab a handful of her blonde hair and pull until her face turns towards me. I'm met with pupils fully dilated, the blue hardly visible, her lips swollen and pouty. I grind to a sudden halt, her mouth curling into a salacious grin. Still holding tightly onto her hair, I jerk back, my dick now hovering just at the entrance to her tight, wet pussy, ready for me to thrust deeply back into her.

What the fuck? This can't be happening. Bang, bang, bang... I look at the head of the bed, but it's not moving.

Bang, bang, bang...

I shoot up in bed, sweat beaded across my forehead and chest. Swinging my legs over the edge of the bed, my cock bounces and slaps against my stomach. It's so fucking heavy and hard that just one tug and I'd be squirting enough cum to keep a spunk bank going for months.

"Fuck, Cannon, I know you're in there." Another bang on the door... but before I can tell him to fuck off, it flies open, and Mammoths huge bulk fills the frame. "Dude cover the junk will you. We all know that you're packing a sizable weapon, so you don't need to put it on show."

"Maybe you should wait for me to invite you in. This is my fucking room after all, and since when have you been shy? Jesus, you're forever getting your cock out for no plausible reason. I was sleeping."

"For your information, I've been hammering on your door for like twenty minutes. You must have been well fucking out of it. With the noises you were making, I thought you had Poison in here with you."

"Like fuck," I bark. "I wouldn't touch her with yours."

Poison is one of the club whores, and her name says it all. She's a venomous bitch who would run over her own grandmother if she had to, especially to get in favor with me. I can't stand the bitch, and she's the last chick on earth I'd fuck. Over the years, she's played some dirty tricks on the other girls, too, meaning they now hate her guts with a passion. If it were up to me, she'd be out of here. Her only saving grace, and the reason she's still tolerated by the other club members, is because my pops has a soft spot for her, or should I say hard spot. She's always willing to please the Pres, to get down on her knees and suck his cock at short notice. Rumor has it that she's got suction stronger than a Shark Navigator vacuum. Personally, I don't know, and I ain't got no intention of finding out either.

"So, who you dreaming about that got you so riled and your dick about to burst? Because I've seen your morning wood before and that"—he points to my groin— "is not just from the usual surge of testosterone."

"Stop looking at my cock. Can't help it if I've got more turbo in my power tool than you've got in your pinky finger, ass wipe. Jealous much?" I snigger at him, trying to evade the subject, because no way am I going to discuss my vivid, inappropriate dreams of Leah. Yep, you got it: it's not the first, and I'm sure as fuck that it won't be the last. Every single one has me waking up with my dick like stone and disgusted with myself for having depraved thoughts of the sexy, hot and stunningly beautiful girl who's too fucking young.

"Why would I be jealous?" he sniggers back at me. "My cock may be marginally smaller than yours, but I have power behind my rocket." He thrusts his hips back and forth, his hands hovering midair as if holding on to an imaginary ass. Jesus, he's so fucking big, he'd have to hold on tight otherwise any real ass would be launched into space.

"You're a fucking idiot," I laugh.

He suddenly becomes serious, a darkness falling over his face. It doesn't last for long before his smile is as big and dopey looking as usual. "Come on, we need to get going. Pops wants us to go check everything at the warehouse before the pickup."

"I'm down to watch the girl," I gripe.

"I've switched you out with Toothpick. He'll keep watch until JB takes over this evening."

"You've sent a fucking prospect? A useless one at that? No, take Buzz with you to the warehouse, I'll take care of the girl."

"Pops wants you on this because it's a new

contact. If this goes to plan, it means a lot of money for the club. He'll go apeshit if we don't take care of it ourselves. Besides, we all know how you want to 'take care of the girl'," He smirks. "But do you really think that's wise?"

I run my hand through my hair, letting out a huge sigh.

"Shit!" Mammoth, sniggers shaking his head at me. "That's who you were boning in your sleep. Young Leah."

"Get the fuck out of here," I growl back at him. He laughs, as he backs out of the room. The door slams shut just before the half-drunk bottle of beer that had been sat on my bedside table, smashes against it.

"Fuck, fuck, fuck!"

I push up off the bed and storm into the connecting bathroom. Stepping into the shower, I turn the water on but leave the heat off, hoping it will cool my ardor. Closing my eyes, I tilt my head into the ice-cold water jets, but it's only a matter of seconds before the image of Leah comes to mind. My cock is still painfully hard, and against my better judgement, I curl my fist around it and take a firm hold. With the memory of my dream still vivid in my head, a dozen swift pumps and I'm grunting out my release.

After washing, I step out of the cubicle and wrap a towel around my waist. Back in my room I reflect over the past few months while I towel dry myself down.

I've managed to avoid all interaction with Leah for nearly a year now, but I've not been able to keep from watching her. She's like a fucking drug, and I need to take my fix. With her eighteenth birthday coming up in a few days and her impending move to college, I'm finding it harder and harder to keep away. Every time I see her, she seems to be transitioning from a teenage girl into a young woman. Her confidence and beauty attracting more and more attention from the opposite sex and some, I've noticed, from the same.

Having a couple of the school kids in our pocket has turned out to be a bonus. Not just so that Leah can be protected from the likes of bullying and drug influences, but also from the horny, spotty assholes that attempt to approach her. Unbeknown to her, there is a strict 'do not touch, unless you want your dick removing with a rusty hacksaw' warning that has been circulated within the school male population, teachers included. Well, it wouldn't be the first time a teacher and pupil had got it on.

No matter how many times I've tried to justify my actions to the club members, insisting that it's simply sticking to the agreement with her brother Sparks, protecting her in every way, they just give me 'whatever' attitude and walk away.

The few that have put this restriction to the test have quickly been given a taste of exactly the consequences if they ignore our warning.

That is until now.

Aaron Brady, Quarterback and captain of the school team: a cocky jock who thinks he's entitled to take whatever he wants, just like his obnoxious, father, who happens to be the brother of the governor of the state of Florida.

The family come from new money gained through real estate, although we're pretty sure that it hasn't been gained legally. It's unfortunate that we haven't been able to prove it because information like that, we could most definitely use to our advantage.

When Aaron made a move on Leah, asking her to be his date to the Prom, I'd made sure that the outlaws stepped in. With his balls in my hands—might I add I was wearing gloves at the time—I'd squeezed hard until I could feel his ball sack protruding between my fingers. With the promise to remove each of his testicles with a butter knife, he'd quickly agreed to forget about the date, and was told that under no circumstances was he to arrange any further liaisons with her. In fact, if he were to so much as get within fifteen feet of her, we'll be back to finish the job. I'd wanted to make it thirty feet, but Mammoth had pointed out that the school hallways weren't even that, so it would have been a near impossibility not to break the boundary I was eager to set.

I've personally kept a close eye on Aaron, but as prom night is tonight, I'm still not sure if the cocky asshole is going to go back on his word or not.

I quickly grab my jeans from the back of the chair where I'd slung them last night and step into them, making sure that I tuck myself in before yanking up the zipper. Plucking a clean white T-shirt from the drawer, I pull it over my head and slip my feet into the scuffed biker boots that have seen better days.

Walking into the main room, I find Mammoth chewing down on a slice of toast. As I walk past him, making my way to leave, he thrusts a hot 'To Go' cup towards me, which I grab before he follows me out of the door.

The quicker I get the warehouse job done, the more chance I have of getting back to stakeout Leah's house and make sure that Aaron Fucking Brady doesn't take my girl to the prom.

CHAPTER FOURTEEN

Cannon

I leave my bike on one of the side streets further down from where she lives and walk to the shadowed spot that I use on a regular basis. It's perfect for viewing the front entrance of her house.

It's six-forty-five, and I'm thinking that if the jock is going to turn up, then it will be anytime soon.

When the door opens and she steps out at the front of the house, I nearly drop my smoke. My jaw becomes slack at the vision of her. The strapless, midnight blue dress that she's wearing is encrusted with what look like rhinestones that sparkle when caught in the porch light. Nipped in tight at the waist the skirt then billows out a little, stopping just above the knee. Even from this distance, I can see the smooth bare skin of her shoulders and neck that seems to glow.

I can't take my eyes off her. She is stunning, mesmerizing and far too tempting for her own good.

A quick check of my phone and I see it's already seven-forty. The Prom started at seven-thirty; it looks like the young douche isn't as cocksure as his persona makes out. Thank fuck for that because the way she looks, I doubt even the weak little shits at school will be able to resist taking a shot at her.

The constant swish of her head looking up and down the street, perhaps unsure which direction her date for the night will arrive from, is punctuated with a quick check at her wristwatch. As time slips further past what must have been the arranged time, her stance became less assured. Her whole-body slumps, her head tilting downwards. Even from this distance, I can almost feel the disappointment oozing from her.

Guilt hits me hard in the chest. She looks so stunning, so grown up, and who the fuck am I to deprive her of her school prom. Doesn't every young girl dream about Prom night?

Against all my principles, knowing this could be a major fuckup, I step out of the shadows and walk towards her.

"Hey," I say when I get to the end of the short

pathway that leads up to the porch. Lifting her head at the sound of my voice our eyes meet.

"What are you doing here?" she cries, the surprise of seeing me clearly evident on her face. It's not long before it switches, though, when she becomes all defensive. She huffs and crosses her arms over her chest. My eyes instantly zone in on her tits which are now pushed together—creamy mounds of silky skin almost bursting over the top of the fabric. Fortunately for me, she's glancing up the street again, no doubt still hoping for her date to turn up. This gives me the time to cover up the fact that I'm perving on her again.

"I was just passing. Saw you standing out here." I flick my half-smoked cigarette towards the storm drain at the roadside, making a perfect shot. "You're all dressed up. Going somewhere?"

"Prom," she mutters, then stands tall before sneering out, "Not that it's any of your business."

She may be pretty, but that snarky fucking mouth of hers has the ability to instantly get my back-up, turning me into an asshole.

"Yeah, someone did mention it was tonight." I mirror her crossed arm pose and leaning up against the gate post. "Where's your date? Running late is he?" I say smugly.

"Go away."

It's exactly what I should do, but I can't help but rile her up a little more. "Shit. If he ain't turned up yet, then I think he's stood you up babe," I say with a smirk.

Before I've had time to blink, she's down the path, going toe to toe with me, her head tilted and all in my face.

"Why don't you just fuck off, Cannon," she spits into my face. "Who do you think you are, the fun police? Every time I'm about to do something I want to do," she stabs her finger into her chest, her voice cracking with the emotional outburst. "You turn up like a cloudburst, and piss all over it, ruining everything. Why can't you just leave me the fuck alone?" As she turns and moves to go back towards her house, I catch her wrist and pull her back towards me. Her eyes are glistening; tears tainted with black streak down her flushed cheeks and her lips part as she gulps in air between sobs.

Instinct takes over and I pull her against me, wrapping her in the warmth of my embrace. She gives in easily, falling against my chest, her hand clinging to the edge of my leather cut.

"Shh, shh," I coo, stroking the back of her head with the palm of my hand. Her long blonde hair feels like silk as it hangs down her back in soft loose curls. I can't resist threading my fingers into it until I can feel the heat of her scalp. "It's okay, Leah, I'm sorry. Please don't cry."

"Why should you be sorry?" she sobs. "It's not like it's you who's bailed on me." She looks up at me with big blue, watery eyes. I have many answers in my head, but not one of them can I offer in my defense, so I just continue to look down at her sad face.

Her lips are swollen from crying and the temptation to lean in and kiss her is mind-fucking. It's like this gorgeous girl is a witch or something and has put me under her spell; it's sucking the life out of me as I try not to succumb to it.

I reluctantly release my hold on her when she starts to wriggle and push against my chest. Taking a step back, she looks down at herself, the pretty dress, the silver heeled pumps at her feet and sighs...

"Such a waste." The disappointment in her voice is clear giving me another punch in the chest.

"Ice cream?" I ask her without even thinking it through.

"Ice cream?" Her eyebrows scrunch together, my question confusing her, but hell it's confusing for me, too.

Gently holding her chin, I tilt it up to me so I can look her in the eye. "Despite me being the killer of all things fun and all that"—I refer to her earlier outburst— "do you trust me?"

When she meets my gaze, I feel like she's looking right into my soul, but however much of a bastard I've been to her in the past, the one thing I don't see in hers is fear.

"I trust you," she whispers.

"Come on then, Ninja Girl," I say, grabbing her hand and linking my fingers with hers. "All is not lost."

As we walk to where I've left my bike, I can't help but think how perfect her hand feels in mine.

CHAPTER FIFTEEN

Cannon

Thirty minutes later, we pull up outside Jenks Diner. It's a small place out of town where, hopefully, I've minimum chance of running into anyone I know because that would be one hell of a fucking nightmare. Not just because, well it would look fucking wrong, but also if one of the Young Outlaws or any other MC club saw me with Leah, I wouldn't hear the last of it.

Once we've both dismounted the bike, I kick out the side stand before turning my attention back to Leah. When I help her remove my helmet that I insisted she wore, I see her cheeks are still streaked with make-up.

"Hey, let's tidy you up a little," I say, holding her

shoulder to keep her still. I lick my thumb then swipe it under her left eye and across her cheek. My skin tingles at the touch sending a message right to my dick, but it doesn't stop me from doing exactly the same to the other side.

"Oh my God," she cries out, bring her hands to where I've just cleared away the remnants of her tears. "I must look a mess."

Taking her wrist, I pull her hands away from her face, keeping hold of one of them. "You look fine." I walk her towards the entrance to the diner and push open the door. "Now, what's your favorite flavor?" I ask when we stand, looking up at the many options available that are plastered on the wall above the counter.

"Strawberry-vanilla. No, banana-caramel. Oh, they have mint-chocolate."

I watch her as her finger taps on her bottom lip, her eyes skimming across the different options. "Eek, I can't decide."

"What can I get you?" the middle-aged server asks. I glance at her name badge before responding.

"Hey Marge, the lady will have one scoop each of the strawberry, the banana-caramel and one of the mint-chocolate," I instruct. "And for myself, I will have two scoops of your finest Madagascan vanilla."

"Take a seat, and I'll bring them over," Marge replies.

The place is empty, so I gesture to Leah for her to pick a booth, and once she slides in across the bench seat, I take the one opposite.

"Why here? Why ice cream?"

"Well, it's not like I can just take you to your school prom as your last-minute substitute date for the night, now is it?"

"Maybe not, but me rocking up with the hot, tattooed VP of the Young Outlaws would have been sick." A tilted smile adorns her lips along with a mischievous glint in her eye. "I can just image Principal Callaghan's face," she sniggers. "Epic."

"Hot?" I smirk, raising my eyebrow in question. My reminder of her description of me has her quickly snapping her attention back to the window, the embarrassment of it all evident in her face. The pink to her cheeks looks good on her.

"Anyway, isn't ice cream the one thing you girls go to when you're got boyfriend troubles?"

"He isn't my boyfriend; it was just meant to be a date," she replies indignantly. "It was the first..." She stops mid-sentence when Marge appears, placing the glass sundae dishes in front of us along with long-handled spoons on top of two bright red napkins.

"Just holler if I can get you anything else," says

Marge. We both voice our thanks before she wanders off to clear one of the tables at the far side of the room.

"OMG! This looks awesome."

I watch her as she navigates her spoon between the three different scoops, taking a bit from each one before bringing it to her mouth. Her lips part, her mouth opens, and the sight of her pink tongue just before she sucks the whole thing into her mouth along with the soft throaty moans of appreciation have my dick jumping in my pants like an overzealous Mexican bean.

Holy Christ strike me down now because all I can think of is how fucking hot she'd look with those pouty lips around my erect cock.

Come on, man. Totally inappropriate.

"I must admit," she mumbles around her spoon. "I'd never have had you down as a vanilla guy."

I raise an eyebrow at her, my lips twitching at the urge to come back at her with some dirty response. Believe me, where my mind is at this time, it's anything but vanilla.

I see the exact moment that the penny drops at her ambiguous comment. Her eyes become wide, her stature rigid and her jaw drops open. The only thing missing is the hand to the mouth.

"I didn't mean... I meant the ice cream... not...

well after seeing... at the club house..." She blushes again. This time she tightly shuts her eyes, and mouths to herself, "Shut up Leah."

I laugh to myself before deciding that the best thing to do to break the current awkwardness is to change the subject. "So, before, you were saying it was the first what?"

A look of relief casts over her face, her body relaxes at my welcomed diversion. "Oh, it was the first time that I've been asked out on a date."

"Really? You've never been on a date?"

"Nope, and I've never made any definite plans for a date before this. A few guys have flirted with me, but then as soon as I've shown any interest, they've backed off." She lets out a huge sigh before scooping another mix of ice cream into her pouty mouth.

Not sure what to say, I just comment, "Weird."

"Maybe I'm doing something that puts them off," she mumbles sadly before she trails her pink tongue from her wrist, and up her little finger, catching the melted cream that had dripped from her spoon.

This was a crazy idea.

"Can I ask you something?" she says with a sigh.

"Sure, but I can't guarantee that I'll answer."

"Am I ugly?" Her eyes are big, blue and fucking mesmerizing.

"What the fuck!" I curse when her words fully register with me. "Why would you think that?"

"I don't know. All the other girls at school, like Dana for example, get plenty of attention. Even the preppy girls get offers from the tech geeks. So, there must be something wrong with me."

"Leah," I take hold of the hand that's still holding the spoon, the one that she'd just tongued, and gently squeeze it. "You are a beautiful young woman. Far prettier than Dana or any of the other girls in your class."

"You're just saying that to make me feel better, besides how would you know what the other girls at school are like?"

"Well I doubt that they would outshine you, and why would I lie? It's not like I've got anything to gain." Shit, that was close. I have seen a lot of the girls she hangs around with, and I do think that she outranks them all, but I can hardly come clean about that now, can I?

"Look, the guy who let you down, we'll it's his loss, and I'm damn sure he's not good enough for you anyway. There are more important things to think about than boys. You'll be graduating soon; you have life choices to make... Why don't you just concentrate on that for now."

"Shit," she laughs. "You sound like my brother."

"Your brother?"

"Yeah, Jordan, and don't pretend that you don't know him," she chides. "You came to the house that day with that other guy: the big hairy dude."

"Mammoth," I inform her before she goes on to tell me how her brother Jordan is so overprotective, and that after losing both their parents, Jordan had become her legal guardian. At least until he ended up in prison. Once she starts, she doesn't stop, but none of it is a surprise to me. I play the game and listen intently, making believable responses in the right places.

Little does she know that I know more about her situation than she does herself. I feel like a fraud, a liar, but not one word leaves my mouth that neither confirms nor denies the fact that I'm deceiving her. But I feel like shit.

Just after she's reminded me that it's been three years that Jordan has been in prison, out of the blue she turns the subject back to me and the club.

"Mammoth," she questions. Her eyebrows come together, and she taps the spoon twice on her bottom lip before she points it toward me. "That's just his biker name, right?"

"My brother, yeah, his real name is Wesson."

"Is he your real brother or just a club brother?"

"He's blood." I laugh at her cheeky inquisitiveness. For now, I'm just glad that the conversation has swerved away from the subject of her brother.

"So, do you have any other siblings?"

"One other brother, Smith. He's Mammoths twin but they're total opposites."

"In what way? Is he four-foot-tall and hairless?" She sniggers before filling her mouth again.

"Not quite," I laugh. "He's still tall but not quite the animal that Mammoth is. He's more the dark, brooding kind and is a total risk taker. He doesn't get involved with the club much. In fact, I haven't seen or heard from him for a while. He's a marine and away overseas."

"Does he still have a MC name then?"

"Brick."

She's looking all confused again. I can almost see the clogs going around in her head. "Mammoth I can understand because, well, he's huge, but where did Brick come from?"

"Long story, short, he had a fight with a brick wall and the wall came off worse."

I don't know why I'm offering up this information, talking so openly, as it's not something I usually divulge or put up for general consumption out of the confines of the club.

"So, how come you got the name Cannon?"

"Shit." I snigger, shaking my head. "I can't

answer that, well not for a couple of years anyway." I wink at her and I know she's put two and two together when her cheeks go that adorable shade of pink.

Fuck, I'm so balancing on the edge of being totally inappropriate again. What the hell am I doing.

"O... kay. So, what's your real name? Surely you can answer that."

"Colt," I reply.

"I like it." Her eyes then suddenly go wide; a soft smile plays on her lips. "Hey, you're all named after guns. That's sick." After scraping around the dish, she puts the last remnants of the ice cream into her mouth. Dropping the spoon back into the empty dish, she falls back against the seat and gives out a huge sigh. "OMG, that was wicked, but I think I'm going to pop," she says letting out a soft moan while rubbing her fabric-covered stomach with the flat of her hand. "I ate too much."

I can't help but laugh, her mood now lifted and her eyes now bright and full of life. Gone is the look of disappointment and rejection. This girl is a breath of fresh air and I just want to breathe her in.

"Didn't you like yours?" she says, nodding to the dish in front of me. I look down to find a pool of mostly melted white goo. I've been so enchanted by Leah; I've hardly touched my dessert.

"I'll just go settle the bill," I quickly sideline, slipping out of the booth. I make to walk towards the counter just as Leah shouts to me that she's going to the rest room. I watch her while Marge rings up the bill. She floats across the floor likes she's some kind of dark angel: a vision in midnight blue. She's a temptation and if she so wished, she could lead me through the gates of hell.

I deserve to be banished to hell with the unlawful thoughts that keep crowding my head.

CHAPTER SIXTEEN

Leah

After taking care of business, I walk over to one of the basins, turn on the faucet and lather up with the foamy soap that I pump into my palms from the dispenser. I let the cool water run over my hands rinsing away the suds. I glance at myself in the mirror, skin flushed, eyes wide, a smile that I can't seem to stop from forming on my lips.

I grab a paper napkin and dry off my hands then deposit it in the trash bin.

Stepping in front of the full-length mirror, I look at the image I see in front of me. The deep blue dress hugs my curves perfectly. My blonde hair, despite wearing the motorcycle helmet, still holds the soft curl that I'd painstakingly practiced over the last few weeks and had finally mastered in time for tonight. The high shoes are incredibly uncomfortable, even though I've been sitting down for the last hour.

I rub my hand over my stomach again, knowing that the weird ache inside it has nothing to do with the intake of sugar but the effect that Cannon has on my emotions. Despite our words, and previous clashes, I can't help the fact that every time he looks at me—whether a smile, a broody frown or a face full of thunder—he makes my skin burn, butterflies in my stomach take flight and mountains of wicked thoughts fill my head.

It has taken all my concentration and will power to make conversation with him, so much so that all I've done is gabble on about my life. I sounded pathetic and so... woe is me. I need to get a grip, but he has this effect on me and it's driving me crazy.

You wouldn't think that being a biker with scuffed up boots and dirty badges on his cut that he'd smell so good, but the musky mix of leather, grease and man is intoxicating. I've found myself inhaling deeply, trying to take in as much as I can, whenever I can. Oh God, I wonder how he tastes, how skilled his lips and tongue are with a kiss. How easily I would give myself up to him, and how far I would let him go... All the way and far beyond my imagination or porn hub fantasies.

The door of the restroom swings open when someone comes in to use the facilities, bringing me back to my senses. I quickly apply a thin layer of subtle pink lip gloss then shove it back into my purse before making my way back to Cannon.

The check paid, I follow him out through the door and back into the warm night air. It's dark now, but the street is reasonably well lit. When I take a step forward towards the bike, he suddenly catches me by my upper arm stopping me from moving any further. When I turn to face him, he's right there, so close that I can feel his breath on my face. For one wishful moment, I think he's going to kiss me. Heat pulses around my body, causing goose bumps to litter across my skin, but my heart freefalls when he takes a step back and averts his gaze.

"There's a park close by," he says, tearing through the awkwardness. "We could take a walk, work off some of that ice cream."

Pushing back my disappointment, I flex my aching toes within my shoes, but not wanting to bring this unplanned and heart pumping experience to an end, I decide it's worth enduring the pain.

"Sure, I'd like that," I reply, but my words and my heart stutter when he takes my hand firmly in his, sparking yet another surge of heat. As he guides me around the corner, down a narrow pathway, we come to a set of iron gates. Letting go of my hand, he turns his back to me and fiddles with the latch. Within no time, he's pulling one side of the gates open, just enough for us to squeeze through. He quickly closes them again. It all feels a little furtive.

When he starts walking, I double step until I'm right beside him, but I feel a little deflated when he doesn't seek my hand again. We walk without talking, and I rattle my brain as to what to say. All I can think is this is so far removed from how I expected my prom night to go. I'd been expecting to walk into the hall on Aaron's arm after having our picture taken by the photographer, to feel the searing heat of jealousy from all the girls that had been vying for the quarterback's attention and the prestige of being his date for the night. I won't deny that I'd daydreamed about the dancing, the fun, maybe even a kiss and the high possibility of getting a little drunk if the rumors had been correct that Jamie Silverson was planning on sneaking in some hard liquor. But despite all that, I can't think that I'd rather be anywhere else than here, right now, with the man who seems to flit in and out of my life, every time leaving his mark on my soul.

"So, what happens after graduation?" Cannon's voice breaks through the silence.

"College. I'm doing a associates degree in science."

"Are you moving away?"

"No, I'm staying here, at least for now."

"Good," I hear him say under his breath. "So, what's your end game?"

"My end game," I laugh. "You mean what do I want to do? My career? That's the million-dollar question. Something in science, but not sure what. I'm hoping I'll wake up one day and wham! It'll come to me in a flash of light. If I'm on the wrong course, then I'll look to switch."

"You're smart, much smarter than I'll ever be."

"I don't know about that."

"Hey, my education was severely disrupted with club life and a father who had no respect for the art of learning or importance of knowledge. Only Brick managed to scrape through and get a GED and that was because he was so determined to become a Marine, not that we knew that at the time."

"You didn't know he was going into the military?" This shocks me as from what I've seen, albeit only limited, he seems to be very close to Mammoth, so why wouldn't he have this closeness with his other brother?

"Brick is a sly bastard, he..."

I stumble in my heels as we hit an uneven piece

of asphalt. His hand slips around my waist and pulls me close, until I regain my footing. Our bodies are so close I can feel the movement of his firm chest and the wisp of air across my face with every breath he takes. Braless due to the dress being strapless, my hardened nipples graze against the fabric, a familiar ache and warmth between my legs identifies my heightened state of arousal.

Tilting my head up so our eyes meet, my lips part as I gasp in air, but my breath is snatched away when his lips cover mine, his hot tongue sweeping into my mouth and playing with the tip of my own. The subtle taste of tobacco muted with a hint of vanilla and mint is divine. When he lets out a deep, husky groan into my open mouth, I don't even try to stifle the moan that bubbles up from my throat.

As he grips my upper arms, our lips part as he viciously pushes me away, and I almost lose my balance. Turning his back to me, hands on his beanie covered head, he strides away from me only to turn and takes a couple of steps back towards me.

"Fuck, fuck, fuck," he grits out between clenched teeth. "Fuck, I shouldn't have done that. I'm sorry, Leah. That should never have happened."

"Why?" I ask, moving towards him, but his outstretched arms, palms facing me, warning me not to come any nearer, have me stopping in my tracks.

"Because you're just a kid, but it's not your fault; I should know better; I'm the adult here."

His words are as painful as a slap to the face, sending my feelings of elation from his attention to utter devastation and humiliation from his rejection.

"Fuck you. You are a patronizing douche bag," I snarl before kicking off my heels. Snatching them up, I turn and start to retrace the route that we've just taken.

"Leah," he shouts behind me, his footsteps slow but precise.

"Fuck off," I throw back over my shoulder. My speed walk slips into a sprint as I take off, ignoring the sting of the harsh surface under my bare feet.

When I get to the gate, I rag at it, pulling with all that I have until it's open enough so I can squeeze through the gap. I run to the corner where I can see the distinctive orange paint work of his bike under the streetlight. Looking back over my shoulder, I can see Cannon has only just got to the other side of the gate.

"So, you think I'm just a kid. Well, I'll show you just how juvenile I can be by stealing the one and only thing that seems to be important to you."

I sprint the rest of the way to his bike. My hands are still full of shoes, so I decide to ditch them, tossing them to the curb. Hitching up the skirt of my dress I straddle the bike. Hands now free, I take hold of the handlebars, lean the bike over to the right and try kick off the stand. I struggle at first, but I have a lot of strength in my legs, and eventually with a sharp, hard flick with my bare heel it comes up. It's only then I realize I can't go anywhere without the keys.

Plan B.

I shuffle to the edge of the seat, leaning and holding on as tight as I can until I manage to kick my leg back, swinging it to the pavement to meet my other leg. As I start to wobble, I let go of the handle-bars and the bike falls to the side. It nearly takes me with it, but I manage to stay upright, stepping back so I don't get smacked around the ankles if it slides. The sound of metal hitting the road makes my teeth tingle. Instantly, a wave of regret washes over me and punches me right in the gut.

"No, Leah, that's my fucking ride." The darkness in his voice is enough to stop my initial instinct to run and has me rooted to the spot. "Don't move. Don't you dare fucking move."

"Shit," I mutter to myself.

Rushing to his bike he takes hold and pulls it upright and puts it back on its stand before circling it to survey the damage. When he looks back at me his face is like thunder. Coming back around to where I stand, he thrusts the helmet towards me and mounts the bike. "Put the fucking lid on, Leah, and get on the bike."

I hesitate, not sure I want to go anywhere with him. He'd been mad that night at the club house when he had found Dana and me there, but this... this is off the scale. He is furious, and I know that this time, I have pushed him too far.

I am pissed too: pissed at him messing with my head, but however much I want to hit back at him, I know it's only going to incite him even more. I don't mind admitting that the Cannon in front of me now is every bit the MC Biker, Outlaw, hard mother-fucker that he is rumored to be, and he's scaring the shit out of me.

"Leah." His deep, low, snarling growl only accelerates my ever-growing fear of what he has planned for me now.

"Where are you taking me?" I breathe heavily, unable to hide the quiver in my voice. "Are you going to punish me?"

"Don't tempt me, Leah. Don't fucking tempt me. Now, do as your told and get your ass up here." He doesn't make eye contact: he just punches the back of the seat behind him with his clenched fist.

Placing the helmet on my head, I tentatively slide onto the back of the bike. I don't want to touch him. Well, I do, but I'm not sure if that will just piss him off even more, but as soon as he accelerates, I have no option but to wrap my arms around his waist and cling on for my life as he takes off at speed.

Most of the way back, I keep my eyes shut and try to take deep breaths to try to control the sick feeling in my stomach. The vibration of the motor between my legs doesn't have the exciting effect it has done previously: it just exasperates my nausea.

I know in the past Cannon has claimed that his odd reactions to me have merely been to stop me getting into trouble, but after what I've done, I'm pretty sure he couldn't give a shit if I was attacked by a pack of lions. I'm sure that the Young Outlaws wouldn't think twice about getting rid of someone for a lot less than wrecking their precious ride.

Is he going to kill me? He is, isn't he? Am I just overreacting? Is he?

I dare not open my eyes incase he's taking me down a dirt track that leads to the swamp. I'd rather not know what my fate is until the last minute.

Will I even get to go to college?

By the time we come to a stop, I'm shaking with fear. Opening my eyes, I see we've pulled up outside my house. Tears of relief teeter at the corner of my eyes, but my inner determination steps forward and I push them back, at least until I get safely to my room.

Sliding off the back of the bike, I pull off the

helmet and shove it back at him with as much force as I can, while he's kicking the bike up on the stand. If it weren't for the fact that he's pretty much made of pure muscle, I'm sure it would have made him lose his balance.

I can't just walk away. Knowing that I'm safe, in familiar surroundings, my bravado has returned, and I have to have my say. Even though I've gone too far, he fucking annoyed me.

"Thanks for the ice cream. Maybe next time, if there is a next time that is, could you serve it without the side order of egotistical, supercilious arsery? Also, don't kiss someone then make them feel like dirt. Oh, and one other thing, it might have slipped your attention, but I'm eighteen in a couple of days, about to start college. I am not a kid, so stop treating me like one."

"Seriously? You intentionally damaged my ride, causing a shit ton of destruction and you think that was the actions of an adult? Your little temper tantrum just proved how immature you are, Leah."

He steps up close, his words hissing from between his teeth as he seethes in front of me. His hand takes hold of my jaw, tilting it up until I'm looking him straight in the eye.

His lips brush the side of my cheek as he moves his mouth to my ear. "So, tell me, Leah." is voice is soft and seductive. "Do you think you're grown up enough for a man to tongue fuck your mouth and squeeze and play with your sweet perky tit, while running his hand up that pretty skirt of yours? What about when a finger slips into your tight little pussy, two, maybe three? Are you sure you're ready for that?"

My lips part, and I try to catch my breath, my body already trembling with lust at his dirty words.

"Well if that's what you're really after, Leah..." He steps back, and instantly, the heat of his closeness is lost. "Then you better grow the fuck up," he growls dismissing me. Turning away he walks back to his bike adding over his shoulder. "Go find yourself a college boy who can break you in, if that's what you want, but don't think for one minute you're ready for a man like..."

"A man like what?" I sneer at him as he slips onto the seat of his bike. Starting up the engine, he pulls hard on the throttle, but before he lets go of the brake and takes off down the street, his stare fixed forward, and he grits out.

"An unlawful man like me."

CHAPTER SEVENTEEN

Cannon

I pull up at the club house but only go in so I can grab one of the 12-gauge, 18-inch pistol grip Mossberg 500 shot guns and a handful of federal eight cartridges before stepping out the back and walking down to the swamp.

I load it up with the maximum five shells and let rip. I randomly shoot, not focusing on any particular target because my thoughts are still on her.

I'm done. I'm so fucking done with that girl, and it's not because of the shit she did to my bike, or Jordan's fucking threat. Temptation is a bitch, and being around her, knowing what she's doing, where she's going, is too fucking much.

I load up again and fire off the five shots in quick succession as I try to work off some of my aggression.

Fuck the agreement. Fuck Jordan. The girl is on her own. I could stay out of her way, let the prospectors do all the watching, but I just know I won't be able to keep my shit if news filters back that doesn't sit right with me.

I admit it, I'm a jealous ass who, despite knowing that it's wrong, wants her for myself.

The hold and control that I want to have over her is disgustingly wrong.

I want to own her.

I want her to be mine.

But I can't have her.

And it's killing me.

So, that's it. It's what has to happen.

The club steps away. I stay away, and I just hope that all this shit doesn't blow up in my face and bite me in the ass.

Decision made; I feel an odd sense of relief as though a weight has been lifted from my shoulders. Things at the club can get back to normal: less drama, an easier life.

As I slide in the last two cartridges, I feel a vibration in my pocket. I let the nose of the gun drop towards the floor and I pull my phone out. It's an unknown number, and while I'd usually ignore it, a dark knowing feeling of dread hits my gut, telling me to take the call.

"Cannon." Mammoth's voice filters through before I've even had chance to say a word.

"Bro, what's going on?"

"I've been picked up by the cops. They're holding me downtown. You need to get hold of Luca Rossi; I think I'm gonna need him."

What the fuck has he gotten himself into this time? Although Luca Rossi is the Club's attorney, we only call him in if any of us, or the club, is in deep shit. Most things can be covered by flashing a little cash.

"You've been arrested? What are they trying to pin on the club this time?"

"Not the club," Mammoth growls out. "This time is all on me."

"What's the charge?" I ask, already knowing that it's not the usual misdemeanor offense.

"Statutory Rape and false imprisonment."

Well holy fuck!

To be continued...
Young Outlaws MC - Justice - Book 2 out soon.

Young Outlaws MC - Vengeance – Book 3 out soon.

If you enjoyed Unlawful and are wanting to find out more about Jordan Sparks and Luca Rossi, then why not try the Damaged Alpha Series.
Universal link: mybook.to/Damagedalphaboxset

ACKNOWLEDGMENTS

No author can do without the fabulous people that are their invisible scaffolding. So, I would like to give them a shout out and uber huge thank you.

Jackie McLeish aka Super Ed - you are my supercharged, bundle of awesomeness.

Nikki Young, my own personal cheerleader and human bra (support).

A special thank you to my pimpets and beta readers: Kirsty Adams, Helen Simpson, Victoria Philpott, Ann Walker, Joanne Edmunds, Lesley Robson, Nikki Robertson, Sarah Van Aker, Sophie Richards, Yvonne Eason and Wendy Susan Hodges. You guys rock.

KL Shandwick, Ava Manello, Tracie Podger, The Indie Girls and all my author friends for their support and many words of wisdom. Each one of you has helped me immensely. Your special people and I am humbled by your kindness.

My reader group - T.L Wainwrights All Things Naughty. Thank you for the feedback and support you have given me. Love you guys!

My family and friends both in and out of the book world.

YOU CAN FIND T.L HERE...

facebook.com/TL-Wainwright-137891269903535

———

www.amazon.co.uk/T.L-
Wainwright/e/Bo12PBC6GC

———

Twitter: @wainwright_tl

———

Instagram: wainwright.tl

———

Bookbub

www.bookbub.com/authors/t-l-wainwright

Website

ttdwainwright.wixsite.com/naughty

Email

ttdwainwright@gmail.com

Printed in Great Britain
by Amazon

81942690R00099